For my children

Aoife, Una, and Eamon

PHILOMEL BOOKS

An imprint of Penguin Random House LLC, New York

First published as part of *Twelve Nights* in Great Britain by Puffin UK, 2018
First published in the United States of America by Philomel,
an imprint of Penguin Random House LLC, 2021

Visit us online at penguinrandomhouse.com.

Library of Congress Cataloging-in-Publication Data is available.

Printed in Canada

ISBN 9781524741648

1 3 5 7 9 10 8 6 4 2

FRI

Design by Ellice M. Lee

Text set in Horley Old Style MT

ARIADNE'S LAMENT

S he had been left on a spit of land, on the edge of an island, in the middle of the sea, deep in winter, far from home, alone: dropped like a story half told.

What good am I?

Kay closed her eyes and wished for someone to come get her. She tried to imagine someone—anyone—who might hear her, someone who could reach across worlds and pluck her from the rock where she had been stranded.

It was no use.

So tell yourself a story.

What use am I, a thing only half said?

So tell yourself a story.

What good, what use?

Tell yourself.

Thoughts crowded her. Reproaches. Kay tried to run the past few days through her head.

She looked out to sea. Her thoughts went in and out from her, uncomprehending, like little waves slapping against rocks. She was the rocks.

She tried to focus on the green and implacable water, the cloud-shade that hung upon and within it, that conferred on it a dull, mineral mystery, like some opaque stone still unquarried and streaked with clay in a cold seat of earth. But her eye—or was it her ear?—flitted without direction from the flat and silent sheet of sea stretching toward the horizon, to the near, kinetic rhythm of the water breaking against the stones of the causeway's rocky head. She was neither one nor the other. Neither the encompassing sea nor the intrusive tide spoke to her in any kind of familiar language.

Again she tried to think through the days that had passed, those few days, those strange and tumultuous days since the night before Christmas, since Christmas morning when she had raised her leg and with resolution placed her heel flat against the frosty slate of the roof outside her window. She had been so resolute, and yet her step had been so light.

As if by a reflex, her hand reached to the ground, its fingers curling to hold that heel, to feel its reassuring tough tendon beneath the skin. She rubbed it, and watched the sea.

The thoughts slipped from her, again, again, again. She had only to look at anything, and they were gone; and how could she not look, when the scene that surrounded her opened to every side like a bleak and awful flower, spread dull like an anvil of cold iron, silent and still, long after the forger's fire had spent to ash?

This is Ariadne's sea, she thought.

"Flat was the sea that Ariadne sailed, when from the monster's bed she cut her way—"

The story came to her easily. It was a simple one. A child was ripped from his father, thrown a slave in chains into the hold of a ship and carried across the sea to be fed to a hideous monster. But all was not what it seemed; for the boy was a prince, his arm was a hero's arm, and the cage in which they threw him—like so much meat—was nothing less than his throne of victory. In the night she, Ariadne, had gone to him. She was the princess of the place, the monster was her own blood, and she before all others knew the secrets of its lair. She: the key, the guide, the deliverer. To the boy she gave a knife.

To him she gave a map of the beast's mazy nest. To him she gave herself; and so, when from the loins of darkness, shedding his bloody toils, he strode again into the harbor's sun-bleached arms, and like a breeze swept onto the decks of his eager ship, she, Ariadne, was the prize he wore upon his arm, the beauty that anointed him new godded among men.

But he had left her. Having no more use for her, he had abandoned her, here, on this island. On this little rock, perhaps, at the end of the long causeway, in the middle of the ocean. Perhaps in this very place. Kay held her sinew tight beneath the skin, and laid her temple upon her knee.

I know her story. Why do I know her story, and not my own?

The answer to this question was obvious. She knew it. She knew it, but she couldn't say it even to herself.

Everything that flowed in Kay's veins, everything beneath her skin, clotted, knotted, and seized up. It wasn't fair. She deserved more than to be left behind, to be lost, to be dropped like a used-up thing.

I know her story because it is mine.

Her father had disappeared—like a light gone out, like a star that winked, and shot, and faded. That had been strange enough, and with her mother's tears, painful. But Kay was never one for just taking it, and when she had woken to noises on Christmas Eve, to the grating of soles on slates, to voices at her window, instead of fear she had come to feel hope. So they had set out over the first, frosty palings of the dawn, she and Ell, trailing down the garden and across the brittle grass behind the long, hastening strides of two wraiths: Flip, so serious and severe, stalking ahead, and behind him—encouraging, cheerful, kind—dear, gentle, shy—Will, a thought or a plan always tickling at the tips of his fingers' touch. In Flip's balloon, all orange fire and lurching, swaying peril, they had risen through the cold morning and let the wind drive them, howling through the stays and rigging, to the east. To the mountain. Kay closed her eyes and summoned to her mind its caves and its quarries, its quiet, shadowy shapes stealing just out of earshot, the wispers weaving through the tunnels of that mountain fastness and, later, across its sheer and scrambled slopes. She remembered Ghast, the horror of his imperious commands and sick, malicious taunts. She remembered how he had taken Ell, and she remembered his hand upon the chain, when to the great library he had dragged, on all fours, a huge dog—but not a dog—

Her memory swerved. Her heart, she knew, was racing.

Down from the clouds she urged it, landing again on the shore as they had landed, in a little plane, skidding over the sands of the coast outside Alexandria. She worked her thoughts down the moss-crusted steps, slipping down the dropping steps of the Alexandria Water Company, ever down into the safety of the cool earth, beneath the flush of the Nile, and into its ancient swamps. There, in some corner of her mind not yet breached by sadness, Phantastes stood on the boards of a broad punt, a pole in his hand, and water, like her thoughts, lapping at its sides. With the touch of her recollection, she traced the five glistening, opal leaves of the lost tree of Byblos—but not lost, not lost—and set her lips to the furled stone secret of the shuttle. Phantastes, like a seer at the heart of a maze, had promised deliverance and redemption. Surely if anyone could find Ell, if anyone could redeem her father, if anyone could help her put her family back together, it was Phantastes.

But there on his terrace, and here in Naxos, all his visions, all their stories, had only come apart again. She recalled Flip's defiance, as he had stood in the door of a little, shaded room, his cheek wearing the shame of Phantastes's angry spittle. And somehow, through the pain in her shoulder, through the delirium of those days, she had glimpsed a greater danger:

Katalepsis, Ghast's double agent and their betrayer on the terrace, stalking them in the harbor, tracking Rex and then fighting him, her hand set against his, pace by pace as in the falling winter light they staggered toward the open sea.

Kay looked up at last, and her eyes locked on the empty pier where the ferry had been rumbling, ready to depart, only an hour before—less—when she had sprung from its decks and raced back to the waterfront. Whatever watery suds once washed in the ferry's wake had by now dispersed and subsided into the slick surface of the sea; Will and Phantastes, too, like vanished surf, were gone—over the horizon, or round the curve of the island's shore. She didn't know. She followed with her eyes the way she herself had come, along the shuttered terraces that lined the bay, then back up the arcing, pebbled spine of the causeway to this forlorn place, this last, bleakest outcrop thrusting into—

The middle of nowhere.

The gray sea knocked at the rocks.

Kay didn't look at it. She didn't look at the still, silent body of the dead wraith, at Rex, who had fallen here, whose head she had held in her hands, whose last words she had felt stir in her hair. There was no grief in her heart, not now, but something worse, more deadly, like the yawning gulf of a blank page that she had not the power to turn. She knew this feeling as fully and intimately as she knew the touch of her own finger to her palm. It was a sense she had known since she had known anything, a sense that walked alongside her throughout her life like a shadow, her other name.

The middle. Always in the middle.

She raised her head to the sky, opened her mouth and did not cry.

1

THE KERMES BOOK

A man in a little speedboat had wanted Kay's attention. The boat had raced toward the island, coming perilously close to it at a very high speed, then banked away, hard, at the last second. Spray had covered the low rocks of the shore with icy water as the boat roared off. Then it had stood idling along the breakwater, about a hundred meters down from the island where she sat. Kay looked out to sea. Now she wasn't sure, in the haze of the horizon's indistinction, if she could still see the ferry, or not. What she could certainly see, and hear, was the police car that had pulled onto the seafront behind her. Its siren had been turned off, but that only meant that someone was about to make the long walk up the causeway to the island where she sat.

Alone, on an island. Alone on an island in the middle of the empty sea. Naxos.

She clung to the name.

Rex's body lay behind her. She had no idea what a policeman would make of a wraith's dead body.

And I don't mean to find out.

Kay kept low as she skirted round to the seaward side of the island, out of view of the shore. She picked her way down to the breakwater and took a few deep breaths while stripping off her coat, the robe she still wore, and beneath it, her shirt and trousers. She wrapped her clothes in her coat, working fast, then tied it into a bundle by crossing and knotting the sleeves. Still taking cartoon breaths, fast and excessive, she slipped without further thought into the freezing sea on the far side of the seawall, holding onto it with one hand as she bobbed in the water. With the other she held the bundle of clothes dry above the surface of the lapping, freezing sea, and began to count off the seconds in her mind. She guessed she had about sixty until she passed out from the cold. Maybe eighty. She pushed herself as fast as she could down the length of the seawall.

At second fifty-eight, the man in the boat pulled her over the far side. "That was very clever," he said. His accent was strange to her, and he didn't smile. "I don't think they saw you." She noticed the thick blanket he had prepared for her, and—huddling low in the hold—wrapped herself in it. The air with its quick wind had sliced her like knives. The scratchy wool of the blanket wasn't much better. As the feeling returned to her skin, the fibrous wool seemed to tear it off in thick, bloody chunks. She didn't dare look, but squatted in the boat, keeping her head down while the man rotated the wheel and slowly, very quietly, drew the boat along the wall and out into open water.

"Who are you?" Kay said. She kept her voice as flat as her body, low, beneath the wind. She recognized him—no more than a boy, really—as one of the dockhands who had been heaving coils of rope onto the ferry as she had leaped ashore. Was it hours ago? A lifetime ago.

"Dionysos," he said. "Someone onshore hired me to pick you up, and catch the ferry."

Flip. So you were watching, after all.

After a few minutes, as the boat tore across the heavy swells, its motor whining into the open air on every crest, Kay unwrapped her clothes from their bundle and wriggled back into them. Her hair was still wet, and in the cold sea air it seemed almost to freeze in thick, snakelike coils. She shook violently every time the boat dipped into the wind, when it caught her where she sprawled on all fours, trying to hold her balance against the violence of the crashing swells, trying to hold her stomach firm in the swells that rocked her with nausea.

"What makes you think we can catch the ferry?" she yelled, over the high roar of the engine and the louder, slapping fury of the waves. Dionysos mimed a telephone to his ear. "The ferry stops at Paros in an hour," he yelled. "I call ahead. It will wait."

He was true to his word. The sun had disappeared into a heavy drift of clouds, and the afternoon much darkened by the time the little speedboat reached the harbor at Paros. Kay's legs, battered by the relentless, vicious knocking of the deck, were covered in wine-dark bruises, but she still had the strength to climb the rope ladder thrown down by the crew over the seaward side of the ferry's vast stern. It was a long climb, but Dionysos had told her to cover the distance as fast as she could, without looking down, while meanwhile he maneuvered the speedboat, in near silence, around the long end of a concrete pier and into the shadows of countless moorings, where it couldn't be seen from the harbormaster's hut. At the top of the ladder Kay wasn't sure whose arms enfolded her, Will's or

Phantastes's—or both. But for a long time, lifted lightly off her exhausted ankles, she dangled in the security of their encircling relief and love, and wept at last her long-pent tears of grief, and terror, and exhaustion.

She could see that the two wraiths, though stricken with sorrow for Rex, were charged to bursting with questions; but they bit their lips within their drawn hoods, and sat to either side of her on the ferry's aft deck, shielding her from the cold and allowing her to shift into a silence like sleep. Hours later, after they had docked in the darkness at Piraeus and Kay had stumbled after them onto the concrete quay, she huddled in the corner of a dingy café with Will while Phantastes arranged a car.

"Who—" began Will.

"Flip," said Kay. "It must have been Flip."

Will nodded, and looked at the table between them. She knew he was ashamed for having doubted his friend, and driven him away.

"Love keeps its promises," she said.

"So they say," agreed Will.

"I promised Rex I would go to his sister," Kay continued. "He said I would find her at the House—"

"Of Razzio," finished Will. "Rex is—Rex's sister is Oidos, the wraith of knowledge in the House of the Two Modes. She dwells in the place of pure knowing. It is to her that wraiths resort, at the beginning, when they first become wraiths. If Rex thinks she can help you—help us—then maybe she can. It's where we want to go anyway. Razzio will help us to find your father."

Kay nodded. A tightness that she had not known was in her, loosened.

Love will keep its promises.

"And he said something else, then—" Kay flinched. "At the end."

Will waited as Kay gathered herself.

"He said that something beautiful was going to happen. He was trying to tell me—he said he saw—but then he—and I don't know what he meant."

Will's hands were still on the table. He looked at them as if they were miles away.

"I don't know, Kay. What do you think he could have meant?"

Just then Phantastes knocked on the wide plate-glass window of the café. His sudden appearance out of the darkness startled them both, and they stood too hastily, knocking the table. Kay's knees, and thoughts, were still jittery as she climbed into the back of the ancient sedan Phantastes had hired, squeezing into its spent springs as deeply as she could. Her mind turned and turned on Rex's words, on the shape of his face as it had floated above hers, at her bedside; at the shape of his face as it had sunk below hers, on the island. She couldn't shake the sense that there was much more to his words than she had understood.

Rex is gone. But Razzio will help us.

At first she couldn't remember why. Surely he had made a pact with Ghast, and would want to stop rather than help them.

But Will said plotting might work where imagining had failed, and Razzio has the greatest plotting board in the world. Two halls could not hold it—but surely Razzio would never plot upon that board to overthrow his ancient ally—

At that moment the driver finally succeeded in starting the engine, which coughed and choked its way into a slow and stuttering rumble all around them. Phantastes had hired the car to drive them to Patras, where they could catch a ferry to Brindisi and drive the rest of the way to Rome. Kay put the thoughts together carefully as her vision finally snapped into place.

Phantastes had assured her that the driver would think the three of them were English tourists. "It's not that they cannot see us at all," he had explained. "It's that they believe the stories we tell them." The smell of diesel and the violent shaking roar of the engine made Kay wish she really were an English tourist and, like the other tourists, wrapped up somewhere warm and quiet. It was so loud, Will almost had to shout so that she could hear him. She was surprised to realize she must have been thinking aloud, because Will seemed to be answering her.

"It wasn't long ago, but you would have been absolutely right. Razzio still loathes Phantastes, that's for sure—" Phantastes turned pointedly toward the dark window beside him, and Will rolled his eyes with affectionate theatricality. "But the partnership with Ghast hasn't quite turned out to be what Razzio expected. For one thing, he thought the festivals were going to continue, only he thought he—"

"He thought he was going to be First Wraith," snarled Phantastes, turning back suddenly toward them. His hand on the edge of the seat was white with tension. "Can you imagine? That pompous right-angled miscreant!"

He snorted as he returned to the window, making a show of peering out into the dark.

"But that wasn't it," Will added softly so that only Kay could hear him. "Razzio would have broken with Ghast anyway. He never intended otherwise."

Kay felt impatience rising in her chest. She didn't care about Razzio's quarrel with Ghast. *Just help me find my sister. That's the only place I want to go.* Kay dug the nails of her right hand into the back of her left. *Six nights.*

The journey went on and on; for eight or nine hours Kay alternately clutched her exhausted stomach and braced her aching back as they swerved and sped up the coast road toward Patras. She dozed, and when she woke she looked groggily out of her window for the white road signs looming out of the darkness, then vanishing behind them: Filiatra, Pyrgos, Amaliada. Every time they turned or came idling to a crossroads, the sedan rattled so violently that Kay's stomach quivered with the motion, and she thought that they might see dawn from a hard shoulder, facing westwards to the sea with a cold wind at their backs. But then the driver would clap his flat palm down on the dash and bark a few stern words, and as if in response the engine would trim up and surge a little, and off they would lurch again, leaving their stomachs several meters behind them.

Somehow—after hours of swerving and speeding,

rattling and at times riding on little more than the wind at their backs—as the long gray light before dawn rose, they pulled up at the pier in Patras. Cold air rushed all over Kay's skin as she climbed out of the car. Will said he would go purchase ferry tickets, while Kay walked to the edge of the pier, away from the waiting cars and buses, and stared at the dark water where it lapped against the cement. Phantastes had followed her, and now stood quietly beside her as she let the rhythm of the sea's ripples strike out a music without meaning.

"Kay," he said. "This may not be the right time, but there is something I want to ask you before we get to Rome, and to Razzio."

She sat down on the bench Phantastes had offered her. For a while they sat together companionably.

"Look at that," said Phantastes. "Have you ever seen anything more beautiful?"

A few lights winked in the darkness beyond where the water broke—how far beyond, it was impossible to tell. At first Kay's eye was drawn to them, puzzling at the flatness of a view that, like a screen, jumbled all its treasures on a single plane. But when she let her gaze drift, she noticed the gathering contours—just suggestions for now, slight intimations of depth and color—which she knew, in time, would throw forth mountains, oceans, skies, all composed of the widest sailing reaches. It was like seeing the oak in an acorn, or the sky in a drop of water hanging from a leaf.

"No," Kay whispered in reply. "It really is wonderful."

"Sometimes the most compelling images are not the colorful images of great depth and full of matter, but the ones that conceal them. Look at this canvas of black—black-black, blue-black, green-black, star-black, sea-black, cloud-black, tree-black, mountain-black. We know these things are there, that they will shortly awaken, but for now they linger in different qualities of darkness, intense and potent. Before us, all you can see is the effacement of what should be—what will be, as the morning wears on—a gut-clutchingly awesome survey of mountains, forests, precipices, valleys, waves, tides and sky. What you see beyond the harbor now is a much more powerful thing. I look out on this water and see expectation, promise, as great a significance as I have witnessed. My looking, here, is a longing."

"So the reality isn't as beautiful, then?" For no reason she could name, Kay felt almost annoyed by the way Phantastes was speaking.

"It is—but its beauty is of midday, and it is a beauty that cloys and stales because it is open. The beauty of night never fades because it is a beauty that has not yet shone, a beauty of hope, of expectation, of desire. Your first view of a midday beauty is always in this sense your last: it becomes familiar, commonplace, indifferent, and thus in time neither beautiful nor really a view at all."

"But then a beautiful thing . . . must always be something you cannot have." *I want to have it. Give me the day. Give me the day at home.*

Phantastes reached out in the dark and placed his open palm against the night before him, as if it were a windowpane. "Too dear for our possessing. Yes, perhaps. But, Kay, do you also understand a different kind of beauty? Maybe I have been too hasty. The beauty of the familiar, of the known; the beauty of home and the fullness of light: these are the beauties of knowledge, and although they frighten me like a rock tomb closing in and cutting off my air, even I can see their power. These are the engines that drive plotting and all narrative—always cycling through the ungraspable present toward a possessable *then*, a time in the past or in the future that can be fixed and held, even owned. The plotters hold them dear. But for me—the image, cloudily wrapped in all its potential meaning, the exalted mist of the present—"

He broke off. The water slapped gently against the pier a few feet below them.

"I am saying too much," said Phantastes. "I only mean that I was too hasty. Even imagining has its flaws."

The gray woolen light had shifted while they spoke. It seemed to clear in patches, drawing away like separate veils, first from this swell on the water, then from that ridge of a distant mountain, first dimming that star, then illuminating that cloud. Kay let the illusions and misapprehensions tease her vision as she watched, imagining a gray form to be the near, hulking prow of a ship, only to be shown moments later that it was the far ridge of a hill. The still scene danced with revelations.

"What flaws?" she asked.

"An image cannot be both known and understood, both seen and grasped," said Phantastes. He spoke slowly, as if carving his thoughts from a block of wood. Kay tried to listen on the edge of his knife. "In the act of imagination we see something, and have a feeling about it, perhaps admire it and enjoy it; but to interpret the thing we see, to understand what it means, we must also destroy the vision. We have to look away to *think about it*. This process happens in time, and partakes of narrative. And so you may say that an imagination is vital, that its image is immediate, that its image is present. But you must also say that the image is fleeting, insubstantial and unknowable. The image is like the now. When is the present moment? Can you ever say, *It is now*? The moment you name the 'now,' it has already gone. And yet we know that it is here, and that it means something real to talk about the present. So it is with the image: the moment you begin to be aware of the image, or of the perception, the imagination, it ceases to be that and becomes the interpretation of itself, of something already lost. So the image, along with the faculty of image-making—the imagination—suffers its own flaws."

In her mind Kay saw Rex's face, still, quiet and composed. Already he was only a collection of brief memories: the night he had trudged through the frost of the parking lot at the Pitt, and held Ell on his knee; the time he had passed sitting by her bed, speaking those distant, incomprehensible words; the long minutes through which he had panted, his head in her hands. Phantastes was right. He was gone now, and all that was left were memories.

And what did he mean?

Phantastes was quiet for a moment or two, as if he were the surface of a water, and swells were passing through him.

"Child, take this and keep it with you."

Kay put out her hand and took a little book. The moment it touched her hand, recognition seemed to rush along her arm as though an electric shock, and in the dim light of the harbor it seemed that she saw and smelled the book's bright-hued leather, heard the rustling of its ancient pages.

"I know this book," she said. The words shot out of her like a reflex. The volume Phantastes had handed her was small; almost small enough to fit comfortably into the palm of one hand. Its supple covers were stained a uniform deep red, and within, she knew, the once-white pages had yellowed. She held it in her hand, remembering, and allowed the obscure shadow of the harbor to conjure her memory of one particular morning the week before.

"I was reading from it on our journey here, while you slept," said Phantastes. He reached into one of the pockets of his robe and drew out a small flashlight. He handed it to her. "Open it at the page I marked. I think it might interest you."

Setting down the light for a moment, Kay opened the book

carefully, with two hands, stretching with the even pressure of her fingers against the tight binding and the stiff, warped block of paper within. Although she thought she knew what to expect, she was surprised to find that, at the point near the back to which Phantastes's bookmark had directed her, the page—and several pages after it—were thickly covered in her father's cramped, heavily inked hand.

"Why don't you read it aloud, child?" said the wraith.

Kay picked the flashlight back up and switched it on. Almost at once, as she began to read, she found she did not need it.

When Kay reached the top of the stairs and stepped across the threshold of the tiny room that perched above the front of the house, her father would be bent over his notebook, writing. The little desk, too cramped for his long, angular legs, might have bucked like a startled dog had he ever turned to welcome her, and upset the morning tea she set carefully by his elbow, just far enough away to be sure that no stray splash would blot his work. It wasn't that he was mean or impolite, she thought as she now climbed the stairs; he was just incurably busy, forever absorbed in one thing or another, and recently so much so that he had stopped eating with the rest of the family. Instead he took cold plates of food (when Kay remembered to bring them to him) alone in this makeshift study. Kay knocked gently on the door with her free hand, steadying the mug in her right as she drew slowly to a moment's halt. She pushed the door open.

The hunched back within the tattered wool of its gray sweater was a greeting she knew well, and one she resented less than her mother did—most of all because she could plainly see, as almost anyone might, just how tense a greeting it was. She put her hand gently on the weary mass of muscle that was her father's right shoulder, and set the steaming tea under the desk lamp, the light of which—against the cold black panes of the window beyond—seemed to drink up its vapor. He said nothing, but then his pen was moving furiously across a line, and without doubt he was in the middle of a thought.

For a moment she paused, all her weight poised on her forward knee, and tried to read the titles on the spines of the books that had been piled haphazardly across the cluttered workspace since the previous night. A few of them were in scripts she couldn't recognize, much less read, and a number of others appeared to be the musty old volumes of Transactions of the Royal Archeological Society that her father often collected from the University Library on his way home for the weekend. But there was one book, sitting at her father's elbow, that she had never seen before. It was of a brushed and faded rose color, not especially thick, and obviously very old. No writing at all appeared on the cover. Though it was a tiny book, it seemed nonetheless somehow broad and flat, but between two of the five raised bands that sectioned its spine, in gold capital letters appeared the simple title "Imagining."

"Katharine—"

I can't keep reading this. I can't stop reading this. Dad.

Kay started as her father looked up from his writing and raised his eyebrows at her. Quizzical, but not unkind. She realized that she was still leaning, now rather heavily, on his shoulder, and pivoted back against the nook created by a battered old filing cabinet that stood hunched against the desk. "Dad, is that a library book—the red one?"

Without a glance or a pause her father answered, "Library book—oh. Of a sort. I'm borrowing it from an old friend." He stared at her for a few moments from a meter away, apparently watching something that was going on at the back of her head. The way he appeared to look through her made her want to squirm.

Dad.

"It's very beautiful," Kay said, awkwardly stealing a glance back at the book and hoping

that she wouldn't have to meet her father's
eyes again.

"Have you looked inside it, Katharine?" he
said. His voice was even, and still very soft.

"No, of course not."

"Would you like to?"

The immediacy of his offer almost took Kay's
breath away. It was unusual enough for her to
get any kind of reaction from her father, above
all this early in the morning—so preoccupied,
so immersed had he been in his study lately. Any
kind of a conversation was extraordinary. But
this staring, this genuine interest—she splayed
the flats of her fingers uncomfortably against
her hips while her father cleared a rough space
before him on the desk. Then, with much more
care, straightening up in his chair as if to stand,
he carefully retrieved the rose-colored volume.
Using both hands, he squared it neatly before him,
brushing his long middle fingers along its edges,
almost with a flourish or a caress, as he laid it
out. Now that the book was closer, Kay could

appreciate how deep and rich the brushed red of its cover really was: it had a gathered intensity that made her think of the vital insides of things, and of her own vulnerability.

"It's kermes," said her father. He spelled the word for her. "The red color comes from a dye called kermes, made from the bodies of insects gathered from oak trees. Only the females are red, and only when they are pregnant. They look like tiny berries. Someone would have crushed the dried bodies into a powder, then boiled it in water to produce a dye, then steeped the leather in it. Once it was widely used, not only for binding books but for all kinds of dyeing and pigments. But today it is hardly known."

Kay leaned over for a closer look, and ran her own finger across the surface of the book's cover, which she found to be much smoother than she had thought, and cool. "It really is beautiful," she said again. "What is the book about?"

Kay's father leaned back in his creaking chair, took off his glasses and rubbed the back of his knuckles painfully across his wrinkled brow. In the indirect, raking light of the desk lamp, the ridges on his face stood out in high relief, like one of the carved, square-set stone faces she sometimes glimpsed on the covers of his books. Replacing his glasses, he sighed and rested the fingertips of both hands upon the edge of the desk before him. He turned his head, looking her full in the face for a second time. His red and haggard eyes glistened even in the low light, and Kay suddenly wondered if perhaps he had been sitting at the desk all night.

"You have seen your mother weaving," he said.

Kay nodded. Her mother had a small loom, and sometimes used it to make pieces of fabric—covers for cushions, little designs. Kay thought of her setting out the warp threads, then taking in her hand the little wooden shuttle, with its bobbin holding a coil of thread, and running it within the warp threads to make the weft, to weave up the little knots that created the fabric. It was painstaking work.

"It's a little like that," he said. "A book of images, made from ideas, like threads, worked across one another."

"I don't understand," said Kay.

"That's not surprising," her father answered. "It's quite difficult, even for an adult. I think I had better show you."

As he pried the book open at its very center, Kay was immediately surprised to discover that, though it was a delicate and exactly made little volume, bound with stiff leather boards, it was not a book but a manuscript, all written by hand. To the left, the yellow-worn paper was blank except for the faint image of ink bleeding through from the other side; but to the right, nearly the entire page was taken up with an ink drawing. A single unlidded eye stared out at her, drawn freely in heavy black pen, but somehow also with exacting detail. From its sides two brawny, gathering arms extended, each of which concluded in a muscular, outsized hand, the palm spread open. It was framed in a large square, within the enclosed border of which ran a linear pattern of entangled leaves. At the right foot of the page several words were written in the same ink, cursively, and in characters Kay was not certain she recognized.

"Is this some sort of illustration?" she asked. "But what kind of story would have this in it?"

"No, it's not a book of stories, Katharine," answered her father. He took up the earlier pages in his left hand and flicked slowly through a sheaf of them, allowing her to see that not just this but every page was covered with similar drawings. "It's a book of emblems—pictures. Each picture is something like a story, except instead of things happening one by one, in a picture like this, everything happens at once. In order to understand it, you need to tell its story yourself."

Kay liked stories, and the weird picture of the staring eye captivated her. "And those words at the bottom of the page—are those the titles of the pictures?" she asked, nearly putting her finger on the writing on the first of the pages, at the center of the book, beneath the leaf-bordered frame.

"Of a sort, yes. You won't be able to make out the words because they are in an old form of writing, and not in English. But if I were to translate this one for you, I would say something like 'Seeing without seeing.' "

Kay paused, thinking it over. "I don't understand what that means," she said after a while. "Either you see or you don't. You can't see and not see at the same time, can you?"

"This particular picture means something, Katharine. Sometimes in order to see what really is, rather than what appears to be, it is necessary to look not with both eyes, but with one eye alone. Looking with two eyes may allow you to see depth and to obtain perspective on the world around you; but it also limits what you may see, precisely by making your view more precise. Sometimes, this picture suggests, you may see more by seeing less, and perhaps you may see in some profounder way by not seeing—in the normal sense—at all."

"But why does the eye have hands?" Kay asked. "Does that mean something too?"

"Right. It is with our hands that we make things, so the hands of this eye work as a symbol of creativity. This kind of seeing, you might say, is about making things. And the eye has no lid, perhaps because such making-seeing requires focus and concentration—you can never blink."

Kay studied the shape of the handed eye for a moment. "Are all the drawings like this one?" she asked. "Do they all mean something? Are they all about seeing?"

"They all mean something, yes, though some of them have meanings I don't understand, or think I don't understand. And no, not all of them are about seeing, though some are. This one"— he turned the page to reveal a drawing of the full moon hanging over a settling ocean—"also represents ways of looking. As the sea becomes still, the water provides a perfect reflection of the moon that illuminates it; the light of the moon is something that the sea beholds, something that the sea itself becomes, and also the very thing by which the two are joined—that is, the light. But it is only in stillness, in concentration, that this union of the watcher, the watched and the watching itself can all become one. And there are deeper meanings to this drawing, but I can only grope at them."

"What do you mean, deeper meanings?"

"Well, for example, there are words at the foot of this drawing I do not understand. They mean something like 'The eye and its double are one.' But there's a pun—that is, the words can mean something else, too, which is more like 'To accuse a friend is to forgive him.'"

The light outside the house was growing paler by the second, so much so that Kay could no longer see her own reflection in the once-black windowpanes before her. In the street a sudden whirring announced the morning's milk delivery. The little truck came to its soft-jolt stop, and sat back on its brakes with a gentle clinking of bottles.

Her father stood by the window, looking into the gem-blue of the east. "And the star will show in the morn," he said under his breath. As if to himself.

"What?"

"Nothing." He suddenly appeared to have noticed the boy shuffling crates of bottles in the street below. "Is that the time—?" Hurrying to the desk again, he seized the little book of emblems, along with a couple of others, and began to cram them into his ragged rucksack. He fumbled with the straps, tightening them, then turned to Kay and tousled her hair, stuck for a moment, it seemed, for something to say.

"You forgot your tea," Kay said.

He smiled, but he didn't have time for tea.

"Is your mum still angry?"

"I think she just wants you to stick around for breakfast like other, normal dads."

He was silent for a moment, looking at a book

on the desk beside him. He tapped his finger on it, so gently that his finger didn't make a sound. "Kay, listen," he said. "I wish you didn't always have to be caught in the middle."

"I'm not."

"I'm afraid this time you are."

The two of them regarded each other for a few seconds. It seemed as long as anything a person might feel or know.

"Kay, remember what I've shown you here, all right? Remember it as well as you remember anything." And then, as if he had reminded himself of a droll joke, he took up the mug carelessly and sloshed the tea down his throat. Kay almost laughed.

"I'll see you later," he said. "Love you." He turned to go.

From the door he turned back. "If you need me, you'll know where to find me. And tell your mother we'll always have Paris. It's a line from an old movie. One she likes."

"She won't like that," said Kay.

"No," he agreed. "But tell her anyway."

And then he was gone. It was the twenty-fourth of December, and the first full day of the winter holiday.

Kay closed the kermes book then and set it on her lap, letting her hands spring away from it a little, as if it were something dangerous or precious. She sat very still and stared at the red brushed cover; at the way in which, despite its plainness, it seemed to create rich fields of intensity and depth, regions of hue that gathered and disappeared as quickly.

"Did my father give this book to you?"

"No, he borrowed it from me on the understanding that he would take care of it. It is one of my oldest paper books, and has not felt the touch of a pen in over five hundred years."

"But he wrote this in it—I mean, this is his handwriting."

"Yes, I recognized it, too."

Out in the harbor one of the blinking lights turned out to have been a little boat all along. It didn't seem to be moving.

"This is what happened the morning he left—I mean, the morning he was taken."

"You remember it, then," said Phantastes.

"I remember it perfectly. Now I do. Just like he said. The morning Ghast took him. It was the last time we saw him at home." Kay didn't dare touch the book again. It was all so strange. "Exactly what happened. It was only last week," she added. She couldn't make sense of the way she had forgotten it all till now; but then, there it was, the clearest memory, as if it had never been gone at all.

Phantastes answered instantly, but as if from a distance. "I thought so. And I wondered then how it was that he could have composed such a history in these words, in this book. For Will recovered it for me from your father's study in your house not five hours later, and gave it to me in Alexandria."

Kay didn't dare breathe but said instead simply, "I don't know." Suddenly she felt very tired again, as if her consciousness were a wave that had run high and splashing over a beach, but then receded into the sea just as fast.

"A mystery, then," Phantastes said. "But I imagine you will have many powerful mysteries in your life; and so I think you should keep the book. It may be that this story will prove an emblem in its way, and grow to be a great imagining."

"All right, you lot," said Will with vigor behind them. "I've got the tickets. Let's go." Coming round the front of the

bench, he brandished the ferry tickets in the air and smiled—
but it was obvious that the smile was an effort, and his eyes
seemed to be looking for something, or someone, not there.

Flip.

Will caught sight of the kermes book lying in Kay's lap.
For a moment a knot seemed to pull tight across his face; and
then he was off again, striding through the rising light, back
toward the line of cars and buses that had begun to shift forward onto the gangway.

Kay looked at Phantastes.

"To accuse a friend is to forgive him," said the old wraith.
He didn't look convinced.

Kay shoved the book into her pocket, jumped to her feet
and ran after Will.

Will barely spoke the whole journey, neither on the ferry
nor after they docked in Brindisi, when the car ran throttling
off the gangway onto the endlessly straight Roman roads slic-
ing across the heel of Italy. Kay watched the low, dried-up fields,
punctuated by the occasional austere majesty of a great pine or
the low, leaf-bare olive and walnut groves. And again, as the
early afternoon sun began to plummet westwards, she picked
out the road signs and, in the failing light, the high towers and

battlements of the ancient cities they passed: Taranto, Potenza, Salerno, Caserta. Everything about the winter landscape seemed bleak, remote, defended, inaccessible.

Where in all of this endless emptiness are you? Where am I? She looked out at the fields and tried not to see them, tried to see what was not there, instead. She tried to imagine how, when the rains and sun returned in spring, these fields would burgeon and flourish with crops, how leaves would clothe the trees and dapple the humid earth with hot shade. She tried to see the barren stubble and hard, cold soil where they passed it, mile after mile, as the promise of all that rich growth and harvest to come. *Absence is a kind of promise, the space that hope takes.* But it was no good. *They're just gone. For all I know, they're gone forever.*

Will occasionally offered Kay dried fruit and cheese, sips from the large water flask, and something that tasted like very dark, bitter chocolate. Phantastes ignored them both, grim and squarely set—probably exhausted, Kay thought, and apprehensive about their destination. At the first signs for Rome he bristled, and by the time the car was fully engulfed in the lights and activity of the city he was practically panting. He spoke to the driver in rapid, curt bursts, and after some frustrated exclamations and startling near-misses, the car pulled through two massive stone pillars, down a wooded lane and, finally, across a wide expanse of perfect grass. The city had quite suddenly melted away, and the car pulled up in front of a massive, stately building with a white stone facade.

"Kay," said Phantastes. They were standing on gravel beside an elegant stone staircase that led up to the building's grand entrance. The car had pulled away, crunching then clattering into the chilly evening. Phantastes stood under an orange lantern that lit the creases of his aged face. "I want to show you something." He dropped to a squat, holding out his hand. It, too, was etched with deep, crevassing lines; and the further it opened, the more distinct those lines became. The fluid movement of skin and muscle was mesmerizing. "An open hand can be trusted. Don't forget that," he said, gripping Kay's shoulder hard and meeting her gaze. "Don't forget that in there."

Kay stood with Will at the foot of the steps as Phantastes rang the bell. She looked at the house. The stairs and door were at the center of a long range of windows across two stories. She counted twenty-five on one side. Grand, palatial sashes, they all stood dark; their wooden trim, once painted, now cracked and peeled. In places the white stone of the facade had crumbled, and the more intently she peered through the thickening darkness, the more she picked out other occasional flaws: rough boards covering a dormer window in the attic, a gutter cracked and hanging from the eaves, a gap in the black iron railing that ran between the gravel court and the building.

Around and above the door where Phantastes stood— growing impatient—was an elegant covered porch supported by dilapidated pillars, bounded by a black, rusted-over wrought-iron railing that ran down either side of the stairs. The steps themselves sagged with wear, and here and there weeds had pushed through cracks. After a night and a day of petrol fumes, lurching, swelling seas and nausea, the falling-down edifice looked just about the way Kay felt. *On the verge of hopeless.* She looked at the steps, and thought she might well find it impossible to climb them.

A short, bald, paunchy man in a black waistcoat and crumpled tie opened one side of the black, two-leaved door and wedged himself into the crack. He spoke to Phantastes in a soft Italian that barely carried on the mild air. Even from behind, the old wraith looked grim and set: the lines carved into the skin at the back of his neck seemed to underscore his determination to see this visit as a spiritual trial. Although his hands hung limply at his sides, his shoulders were square and rigid, and his eyes, Kay thought, would be piercing. The other man, by contrast, looked calm and unflappable, languid as if on the verge of sleep, as slow to rouse as the oil that seemed to suffuse his olive complexion, and entirely unconcerned by the sharp interjections Phantastes fired at him. On and on they quarreled, till at last Phantastes flung up his arm and threw himself at the door, battering it open just enough to sweep into the house behind the waistcoat—the waistcoat who didn't look behind him as the old wraith passed by, but rolled his eyes theatrically.

"*Che brutto,*" he announced, and frowned. Then, putting his hands together before him and inclining his head slightly as if about to pray, he turned to Will and Kay as they reached the top of the stairs, and said, smiling, "*Guglielmo, benvenuto.*" With a flourish he bowed, turned on his heel and strode back into the house, leaving the door, with its flaking paint, standing wide open before them.

Dusk was gathering fast in the gravel court that lay before the house, and beneath evergreen trees to one side, pools of darkness among the boughs seemed to ripple outward. But Kay would have taken any of those trees over the impenetrable gloom that waited beyond the threshold of the house before them. She stood stock-still.

"Kay," said Will. His voice was soft. "That book—"

"Is mine," she said.

"It's strange," Will offered.

Kay slipped her hand instinctively into her pocket, where the book lay wedged close to her thigh. She thought of her father's wisdom tooth, so many days before.

"Look after it," Will said. "That's all." He gave Kay a wink, picked up his sack and skipped over the threshold, seeming lighter than he had in all the days she'd known him. She watched him disappear into the dark hallway, and willed herself to pick up her feet and skip as he had done, to take on this new place, this new chance with hope. He truly was—what was that word Phantastes had used?—*resilient*.

Maybe this is his home, but it's not mine. Kay looked at the scratches on the backs of her hands. She had made them herself, all through the long night. Each line on her skin was a path to somewhere.

And then she saw that she had made two fists. She fanned her fingers wide, feeling them ache as they stretched. *An open hand can be trusted.* Then she crossed the threshold herself, and shut the tall, heavy door quietly behind her.

As he ranted, contorting and squeezing the muscles in his neck and shoulders in order to push every liquid ounce of available blood into his purple face, he wondered for a moment whether he was not in fact frightened. He certainly sounded it. His voice touched a high pitch of fury that could only be explained by fear. He saw that the assembled plotters knew that. He watched them from behind his performance. And he watched his performance. He had practiced it, then run it over in his mind for hours while the barge drifted down the river toward nightfall, so often and so thoroughly that it flowed from him now without effort. He was not frightened; but it was a measure of the quality of his performance that even he should doubt himself.

He had killed. He would kill again. In the mines below the mountain, after all, he killed every day. Stories began; why should they not end? To kill was to tell the story of another's end, nothing more. This did not trouble him. What is more, he was ready to accept his own end whenever it should come. He knew the common signs for which he should watch—the foreboding, the dwindling power, his own overreaching—and knew he would recognize them with pleasure when they appeared. That was as it should be. No, neither the thought of his own death nor that of anyone else troubled him.

But improvisation. Improvisation troubled him. What that wild knife of an imaginer might do. Might have done. Surely by now he was dead.

He removed his thick woolen undercoat, hung it on the peg provided and began to unbutton the long cotton tunic he wore next to the skin of his arms. He always removed his tunic in the same manner, always noted that he did so and always took pleasure in the observation. There were seven buttons, and thus several thousand distinct patterns in which he might attend to them. He had passed a great deal of time in his childhood experimenting with them until he found a sequence that pleased him. For his own reasons.

The skin of his arms was sacred to him. No hand but his mother's had ever touched it. She had been dead many years, but he still remembered her stroke sweeping over the downy light hairs of his arms, as if to start a story. With a single delicate motion he drew first one sleeve then the other down the length of his shoulder, past his elbow and at last off his forearm. The air in which he stood was freezing, and he watched with pleasure as the taut pores of his skin reacted to the suddenly dry, icy room. He closed his eyes and felt the stroke of cold passing down his arm to his wrist.

No body could refuse that stroke. It made no difference what was in the mind, what vain imaginations frothed there. The body was mechanical, an instrument of cause and effect. Lying, dying on the stone somewhere, his blood leaching out into the earth, draining his corpse of its latest warmth—that was what the great improviser himself would have felt: the slow stroke of a cold hand passing along his arms, touching him lightly at the wrists and letting him go. He could not have resisted it. He did not resist it.

The body was mechanical, an instrument of cause and effect. He smiled. It had taken two hundred wispers, another hundred wraiths, give or take a score, and the combined administrative might of the whole of the Bindery to do it, but he had done it: he had proven, and by experiment, that the much-vaunted imagination of a human child—the very bed and heart of what people naively called "humanity"—was nothing more than a piece of clockwork. Flood it with sensations, and it would seem to flourish and create, for the play of imagination was nothing but the mechanical decay of past sensation—now remembered imperfectly, like images on a broken mirror, now dispersed, scattered, recombined and, in time, lost. Deprive it of sensation, and the imagination would fail. Twist and batter it with ugliness, and it would grow deformed. Betray it utterly, and it would die, taking the whole body with it. The cold stroke of it, sweeping up the arm, which no one could resist.

The journey down the river from the mountain to the sea was also pleasingly mechanical, and told a story of gathering necessity. Ghast took the heavy blankets one by one from the chest of drawers where they had been laid out for him, and gathered them around his squat frame until he stood like a king in his robes, alone in the center of the dark room. The bed waited before him, a great carved stead that had borne the weight of countless imaginers, cradle to their fantastic dreams. Grotesques and gargoyle faces, a seemingly endless trailing vine of floral exuberance mingled with human, animal and other forms, caught the scant gleams from the windows. He knew it would be a sacrilege for him to sleep in this place, to defile with his murdering arms a seat of so much fabled power. For a plotter to sleep in the bed of dreams.

He climbed into its hold. He knew he would not dream.

2

THE HOUSE OF THE TWO MODES

K ay stood in a large lobby. Below her feet, stone
mosaics marched, turned and swirled in relentlessly
geometrical patterns, through a muted riot of color
and shape. The walls rose steeply about her, high into a gloom
above, from which descended a huge crystal chandelier—unlit
and dusty, like the brittle body of a dead spider still dangling
from the far corner of a ceiling. At first, Kay took the walls to be
blank expanses of smooth cream stone, but as her eyes adjusted
to the interior light, she saw that they, too, threw out texture and
shape; etched arcs and circles, eddies and spirals that reminded
her of the way Will's hands worked on the board, or in the air,
whenever he was plotting.

Will and Phantastes had long since disappeared some-where into the building beyond her—through one of three doors that led from the room, one in the center of each of the walls that divided her from the inside of the house. She had stopped in the silent darkness, unsure of which door to take; and in that moment of catching her breath, catching at her own steps, Kay caught herself, and began to notice the loud and tumbling beauty that seemed to plot the space around her. The patterns on the floor and walls moved with such energy that at first she felt her own voice rising up in her throat, as if they called for an answer or would spur her into song. But then she felt something else instead as she noticed how the flow of movement, as it worked along the edges of the floor, of the walls, of the room, into the corners, held to its line, graced and flirted with the edge but never crossed it. All at once, like a sigh heaving over and coming to its long rest in her thought, Kay's stomach settled and she subsided into calm.

Maybe Will is right. Maybe this is *a kind of home.*

Kay turned to the right and approached the door. From the room behind it, through the cracks that ran around the frame, light was pressing its slender fingers into the lobby. She put her hand to the round brass knob. It turned easily. She pushed.

What lay behind the door immediately surprised her with its size and brilliance. Its scope. Like a grand salon from a fairy tale, it glittered with a luminosity that moments before she could not have imagined; from the high ceiling hung lamps of every kind, from simple round and visored bulbs, to shaded and cupboarded lanterns, to the grandest glass and iron chandeliers, every one shouldering its neighbor, each throwing out its shard or pool or shaft of brilliance. Up and down, all the lights rebounded and shot around the walls, which were lined on three sides with what seemed like a hundred grand and gaudily decorated mirrors. Kay's eyes raced with the light, scattering and glancing from surface to surface, and it was several seconds before she realized that she still had the brass doorknob in her hand, that she was still standing in the entrance. She closed the door behind her, let her feet shuffle back up to it and leaned against its solid reassurance while she tried to take in what lay before her.

Apart from the mirrors, and the great glass windows that dominated the right-hand wall, the room was nearly empty. An elaborate purple sofa, long and plush, stood in its center, facing her, and beneath it lay a huge, vibrantly scarlet Persian rug. Elsewhere the floors were wooden. So were the two ornate, gleaming cupboards facing each other from opposite walls at the far end. Nothing moved but the light, and Kay suddenly realized that, for all the warm yellow glow bounding and rebounding in her eyes, the air was extraordinarily cold. Her arms crossed, rubbing her shoulders, she set off straight through the space toward an open door in the far wall, and slipped through it.

The next room was much the same in shape: along the right wall a tier of stately windows towered from floor to ceiling, where a cornice and cast friezes ran in white plaster against the corners; at the distant end of the room another matching door faced her, and in between, in all the inward vastness, there was very little. But this room was only dimly and intermittently lit, by a wood fire that roared in a huge grate to her left, and—beside it—by a tall, elegant standing lamp with three delicate shades shrouding three glowing bulbs. Beside the lamp stood a winged armchair, and to its left a low table, on which there lay a book. Along the walls there were three other tables, none of them very elaborate though all of marble; on one lay another book, on the second stood an earthen pitcher, and on the third was a woven basket full of ripe apples. Kay crossed to the apples, took one and held it up to her nose. It smelled distantly

sweet. She bit into it, and found the flesh sharp, crisp and soaking with juice. While she chewed, she pictured this room from
the outside of the house, counting down the windows, scaling it
against the exterior.

*There must be twelve of these rooms on either side of the
front door, each alike.*

Taking the apple, and neglecting now to close the doors
behind her, she strode from room to high-ceilinged room, finding it exactly as she had thought—each the same shape, each
decorated, although sparely, in a different way, making an
entirely different impression on the senses. In one she found
nothing but ten grand paintings hung in ornate gilt frames, and
for a moment she thought perhaps she was in a museum.

In the next she almost stumbled as she entered, trip-
ping over dice—innumerable dice of every color and size and
material—strewn across the wooden floor in every direction.
She picked her way through them, trying to dodge the thousands of paper butterflies strung from the ceiling on lightly
elasticated cords, so airy and insubstantial that her very being
caused them all to shiver and flutter, and the wind of her breath
and her passing sent them gyrating and fluttering in rippling
waves of chaos all around her. In the last of the twelve rooms—a

corner room—the great windows stood to the right, and again on the far wall; she turned the offered corner, taking a door to her left, and continued resolutely on, passing through space after space, each one different, each one the same.

And then everything changed.

As Kay opened the third or fourth door on this new row, the eager and intrepid spirit with which she had raced through the house, the wonder with which she had encountered its novelties and oddities, vanished. Before her, as the chiming of an antique clock tolled in her ears, sat an old wraith on a carved wooden throne—bulky, gnarled, taut; in places twisted, formidable and severe. Her hair, a blend of wax and ash, rushed around her face, drawing in the eye, drawing Kay to her as the door slipped softly onto its latch. Each of her knowing eyes lay nested in a dense tangle of creases and hatchwork, lines texturing her haggard, hard skin, but cutting deeper, too, as if her skin, her lips, her eyes, had been hewn from bone. She wore a simple gray robe that covered her long, folded body. Its hood lay massed behind her broad shoulders, and from its wide sleeves the wraith's tendons, clothed in rough amber skin flecked with age like a snake's, gripped firmly the arms of the throne.

Kay found herself walking toward this wraith, this throne.

This throne: the high arms tooled with hammered gold; ridges and veins of wood circled those of gold, and together they arced and darted into the forms of eyes, suns, snakes, arrows and swords. Kay, whose own eyes were about level with one of these turned arms, felt her stomach give way a little as she caught sight of a particular carving—a gold sword cutting down through a mass of serpentine. Some thought was pressing at the back of her mind, but she had no time to attend to it, because she was too near, because the old woman suddenly leaned forward and, with both knotty but slender hands, took hold of Kay's head.

"Girl, do you know who I am?"

"You are one of the two modes," Kay answered. *Whatever that even means.*

"Do you *know* who I am?" she repeated—only it was not a repetition, because this time Kay heard the question differently, in the same way that, if you lie quietly, listening to your regular heartbeat or a watch tick, you begin to hear a rhythm of stresses. The stresses were screaming in Kay's head.

What am I doing in this place?

"Yes."

The old woman's eyes, staring down at Kay, never softened, but she let Kay's head drop and returned to her previous posture. With unhurried and deliberate gravity, she laid her arms along the arms of the chair. In the long silence Kay shuffled backward a little, all the while looking closely at those hands resting on the pommels; they reminded her of the hands of someone she had seen recently—but where? As she tried to think back over the confusion of the last days, her eyes drifted to the chair's inlaid carvings, and the two thoughts suddenly merged in her head.

"Oh," she said aloud. "Rex. You have the same hands, and the same symbol of a snake entwined with a sword."

"You did not realize how much you knew," said the mode. "How much else do you know, without knowing that you know it?"

"I know a lot about how little I know," Kay said. "Especially when it comes to the last few days."

The old wraith said nothing.

"For example," Kay went on, "I want to know what I'm supposed to do here. I don't know. I want to know how to get my family back. I don't know. And I want to know how to go home. How do I go home?"

Still the old wraith said nothing. She was looking, Kay noticed, at her own hands. After a few moments her right hand crossed to her left, and she began, very self-consciously, to rub the large gray-blue veins standing proud behind the angular ridge of her knuckles. Kay thought of the scratches on her own hands, and hid them.

"Rex was my brother," said the mode. Her voice lay as quiet in the room as a woven mat lies upon the floor, and as still. "Rex and Oidos, twins in body, twins in thought, two children of the same heart, each the home of the other—till Ghast destroyed him."

In the afternoon of a searing summer day the heat will sometimes hang thickest and most oppressively long after the sun has reached and passed its height. Here, Kay thought, was pain without glare, a long afternoon of sorrow.

"Has Phantastes been, then, to tell you about what happened?" Kay said, still timid before this enthroned old queen.

Oidos looked up from her hands to Kay's face. Her expression was almost kindly. "No, child. Ghast destroyed Rex many years ago. What happened on Naxos we all foresaw: the inevitable roll of a distant thunder. But the crack that made that thunder, it is long gone. Ghast is shedding what he thinks is the corrupted blood of a diseased body. He hopes to purify the present by freeing it from the contamination of the past, enlarging it from the prison of its own history." She stopped, and her right hand seemed to hover and draw like a magnet to cup Kay's cheek. "I did not think you would be so beautiful, Katharine. Razzio and Ontos promised a pearl, but I think you have more of the diamond about you."

Kay would have flushed at the praise had she not suddenly felt so confused. First Will and Flip had thought her what it turned out, in her stead, Ell was—the author. It was Ell who would join the wraiths; *she* could not. But now Oidos was talking as if Kay mattered; and she realized with surprise, and with crushing embarrassment, that she wanted to matter, wanted it more than anything else she could think of.

Who am I?

But she didn't dare think about it.

"This is his room, you know."

"His room?"

"Rex's room. Stand beside me, and see what I see."

Kay took a place to the left of the high throne, and turned. Looking back toward the door through which she had entered, she saw a wall lined with statues: on the left, standing in the corner, a giant form cut from white marble—goat below, from the torso a rippling, towering man, his great beard parting on a godlike face, its roaring smile breaking like the sun from a storm. Rearing on his hind legs, with the two forward hoofs splayed as if readied for battle, he seemed at once startled, fierce, proud and potent. By his waist in his right hand he gripped a horn, carved with such delicacy and precision that it seemed for a second as if he might lift it to his lips and call them both to the hunt. Kay almost stepped back.

"Sylvanus," said Oidos. "The first form taken by the Primary Fury. In the early days of the Honorable Society, when the world was young and the Society's members gathered in wild festivals under the full moon, it was Sylvanus who heralded the beginning of our sacred rites. On his horn he blew the music that frenzied the mind, and dissolved the limits between us, the terrifying dissonance that shivers and breaks down all boundaries, flowing like excess itself across thought, feeling, person, perspective. In the hearing of that music, we came together as one; we were unified in a single chorus as elemental as the earth, as potent as the sea, quick as the flame and boundless as the air. Those were the days of blood ritual and sacrifice, when nation fought nation in terrible battles, and stories were sung in the war camps and in the mead halls, when the bards were kings and their verses spun richer than gold."

Kay shook, whether from fear or excitement she wasn't sure. The white marble form seemed not blank but imminent, as if it might instantly bloom with color, burst into motion and plunge them back into its wooded, moonlit, violent world.

"Look again," said Oidos, extending her right hand to point toward the door through which Kay had come.

Above it—again, carved in white stone—she saw another form, this one a form she knew. Standing not in the porter's uniform of black wool in which she had first met him, but in the long robe that Oidos herself now wore, his arms hanging not limp but ready at his sides, and his face not quite as old as she had known it, but still recognizable—ruddy, square-set and solid like the trunk of a tree—was Rex. In his right hand he carried a ring from which dangled a collection of keys; keys she recognized, each one a distinct shape—square, circular, triangular, with various tines and edges cut against their several shanks. She tried to study his face, the face in which the sculptor had captured him, but whether it was an effect of the white marble, or something true to his form and likeness, she found her eye incapable of lingering on his cheek, or nose, or mouth; it was drawn inexorably into his gaze, into the blank, white, wide portals of his eyes, as open and encompassing as the level stare into which Oidos had, moments before, also drawn her.

"The Wraith of Keys, my brother, Pyrexis," murmured Oidos. There was no mistaking the grounded affection in her voice, that soft tenderness with which love reverently handles its beloved. "Pyrexis, fury, the fever in which the horn is sounded, that like Joshua at the walls of Jericho bursts the doors from their frames and lays open every heart."

"And the third statue?" Kay pointed to the right corner of the room, where what seemed to be another work in stone stood draped with a heavy white sheet.

"Sylvanus was the first form, Rex the second. The past stands behind and open to us, the present is the door through which we come and go, but the future remains shrouded in its own darkness. Time may or may not reveal what lies beneath that shroud. Rex himself never knew."

"Did he come here?"

"Yes, my child. Here in the place of pure knowing, in the House of the Two Modes, all wraiths come to find themselves, to read their own story. This is Rex's room, and it was to this room that he often resorted for contemplation and for self-study."

"And are these his things?" Kay turned, searching the

room. In addition to the three statues, she saw—at the room's other end—a tall, elegant, circular table on which stood an hourglass, the sand heaped at its base, and a large but fine-toothed comb, carved perhaps of some kind of bone; beneath their feet a woven carpet covered most of the huge room, its dominant colors purple, blue, red and white, so that it pulsed in rich arteries of hue that burst, here and there, into pools of dense, throbbing intensity. It mesmerized the eye. There was the throne, and beside it a lamp. On the wall hung four large paintings, two to either side of a huge, empty hearth. On the mantel stood several small objects: a gilt book, an empty silver candlestick and a little ball about the size of Kay's fist, covered in a silver netting or lattice, and containing what appeared in the light to be pure gold.

"Each room in the place of pure knowing contains a collection of twenty objects and elements. Each wing of the house contains—"

"Twenty-five rooms, counting the lobby," Kay said.

Oidos smiled. "Very good, child. Very good. But in addition to the front of the house, there is another set of rooms in the rear. There is also another story following the same plan, and a single room in the eaves."

"So—" Kay mapped it in her mind, as if she were counting on her fingers. "Razzio's house has a hundred and twenty-five rooms!"

"I think you turned a corner to reach me?"

Kay paused. She remembered the corner room. But—

"The House of the Two Modes is arranged in a square, child."

Kay stepped sharply away from the throne, suddenly aware of the vastness of the palace around her.

But that's five hundred rooms. And if each room has twenty objects, then that's—

"Ten thousand things."

A house of ten thousand things.

"And each one of these ten thousand things has its meaning, and those meanings hold the secret of a wraith's identity, or in most cases the identity of several wraiths—for many things have more than one meaning."

Kay shook her head as if erasing everything from her mind. "I didn't count twenty in this room," she said. *I counted seventeen. Including the carpet.*

Kay met Oidos's eyes, and from within the deep, hard sadness of her face the wraith seemed to smile. She lifted one of her hands off the arm of her throne—Rex's throne—and from within her robe withdrew something and opened her palm.

Upon it were two minutely carved pieces of stone, almost as small as jewelry, but worked with such precision that Kay thought she would never tire of peering at them. Black as obsidian or the night, they gleamed in Oidos's open hand, where they caught the light from above. One was a miniature sword, with a slender blade rising from a decorated, two-handed hilt. The grip had been carved with such care that tiny lozenges reflecting the light seemed to spangle like diamonds, while the blade—though not more than a few centimeters long—bore a tiny cursive inscription. The second piece was a sort of helix in the shape of a writhing snake, its coils so intricate, so flawlessly hammered, so exact in every particular, that Kay felt tears start in her eyes. She knew without looking that the blade of the sword would slide easily and completely into the helical void around which the snake's body turned.

"They're so beautiful," she said. "Do they have a meaning?"

"There is nothing in this world that does not have a meaning, because everything in this world is either caused or causing."

"Then what does it mean?" Kay pushed the sword in Oidos's

palm, trying to make out the inscription against the light.

"What you see as the blade of the sword is the space where you do not see the snake, while what you see as the snake is that which is revealed by the blade around which it twines. Both of these things exist: the sword that signifies action, and the snake that signifies thought. But we would know nothing of one without the other."

"So this symbol is about thoughts and actions? It means that you can't have one without the other?"

"It means that you cannot know one without the other. An action is defined by the thoughts that guide it and make sense of it; similarly, a thought is only expressed and made real by an action."

Kay nodded slowly, trying to make sense of what she'd heard. "Why do only some of the wraiths carry things with this symbol? Rex had it on some keys, and Will and Flip had it—it was on a card they left for me, on my bed, the night they took my father from his office. That woman in his rooms at St. Nick's—she had it, too."

"They all carry the badge of the left-wraiths because they are all left-wraiths. That is, they are all left-wraiths *now*."

"You mean Will."

"Yes, child. He was not always a left-wraith—or, to be more exact, he was not always treated as a left-wraith. Really he is no more a left-wraith than you—" Oidos broke off abruptly. The roots of Kay's hair suddenly burned, as if each of them were an ear straining after a distant voice. The old woman stroked her left hand again purposefully, and then went on. "But, child, this is beside the point. Ask me the questions you have come to Rome to have answered."

Kay started, as if she had been tricked by a mesmerizing illusion, and then had it all snatched from under her nose. She had become so entranced with the room, its things, its forms and ideas—

—that I forgot the very things that make me who I am.

She took a deep breath.

"I want to know how to find my father and my sister. I want us all to go home. Will you help me?"

Oidos closed her palm tightly over the black stone ornaments and stowed them inside her robe again. She grasped the arms of the throne and turned her head to face the door. Kay thought for a moment that the old wraith might now refuse to speak at all. But her face was not set, and her eyes looked not severe but pensive.

"You must go out into the garden," said Oidos at last. "You must be yourself, my daughter, before you can know yourself. Go out into the garden and, when you are ready, return, and I will help you." With a great effort that revealed not frailty but, it seemed, exhaustion, she got to her feet and took Kay's hand. Together they walked through the room, through the door, and another door, and another, until soon they stood in a lobby very like the one through which Kay had first entered the house. Here Oidos turned, leading Kay into the back, to another grand hall that opened through enormous glass doors into the garden beyond. Kay glimpsed a vast court, paved in places with stone and cobbled paths, in other places covered with vines or grass. Wraiths swarmed everywhere.

"If you return, I will show you what you need to see," said Oidos, putting her hand to the door that led to the garden. "For you, too, have a room in the place of pure knowing."

With those words she opened the door, and a wave of noise and life and exuberance and pleasure flooded into the room, so thick and warm and irresistible that Kay hardly needed Oidos's gentle push, and instead tumbled over the threshold into the garden, and spun and spun and spun in wonder at the tumult and pace and sudden overwhelming vitality that surrounded her. At first she had simply impressions: a glowing magnolia light, punctuated at swift intervals by a painfully brilliant beam of glaring white; a whirling of outsized motion; the hot, moist air, like the soggy humidity before a summer storm, billowing upon her face; a carnival noise of horns; and a soft pile beneath her feet which, looking down, she saw was grass.

She was still blinking and dumbfounded when a body slammed into her from the side, sending her stumbling. She might have fallen but for the arms that caught her in their warm embrace—half laughing, half apologetic, it was Will.

"What is this place?" Kay shouted back, drilling her eyes as seriously as she could directly into Will's chin.

He had been grinning like an oaf, and the words seemed to burst through his smile without making any impression on his face at all.

"The House of the Two Modes, Razzio's garden, the largest and most complex plotting board in the world, the place of pure being!" he said.

Kay could barely hear him over the cacophony. A column of trombonists snaking round from his right pushed their way directly between them. She flattened herself against the door and looked about while Will, still grinning wildly, followed the musicians, shimmying along behind them. He couldn't stop laughing, and Kay found that she couldn't stop smiling, just to see it. Entirely wiped clean, at least for now, were all the hours of anguish and waiting; the long, groggy stretches in the Pylos pension; the everlasting night and day of the journey across Italy, with its weird moonlit shapes and surprising, nauseating bends. She felt the intensity of her conversation with Oidos slipping from her, too, like a shore retreating as her little boat started to toss on Atlantic swells.

For a few minutes she drifted without purpose around the huge but inviting open garden, surfing its surges, taking it all in. Here, as a group of animatedly chattering men in long tails strolled out of her path, she happened upon a great oval fountain surrounded by a pool of shimmering water; just beyond it, her fingers still cool from the fountain's water, she nearly collided with a column of waitresses filing across the lawn bearing huge covered platters in hefted hands; yet further, a row of children sat on a row of chairs, gripping jacks in their hands as they watched the game of two older girls; there, further on, in among some bushes, a man reclined on a chaise longue, fantastically exotic birds perched all around him, singing to them in a melody of clicks and warbles. In one place she paused for some minutes just outside a circle of poorly dressed men and women sitting on the grass, who seemed to be debating some question having to do with plotting boards; with delight Kay watched agile and expressive hands describe in the air the perturbations of their thoughts. In another place she found the trombones, no longer snaking but still belting out their brash lines in a huge and deafening horn section, itself only one part of an orchestra, apparently being led by a tall man atop a podium, his hands milling in the air. Will lay sprawled among the trumpets, his feet still tapping out the inescapable rhythms.

Kay crouched at his ear. "Is that Razzio over there?" She pointed. "The one leading the orchestra, I mean!"

Will goggled at her, then just shook his head wildly; but, seeing that this was only going to prompt her to further questions, he climbed to his feet and motioned for her to follow. Through the presses of people and the profusion of obstacles— tables, chairs, bushes and trees, more fountains, little grass huts, here and there a canal—Will led her purposefully until, drawing up under the shade of a trellised grape arbor, he ducked gracefully into a corner and sat lightly on a secluded bench. Kay sat beside him, taking in with relief the now muffled fanfares and muted roars of conversation, while she perched in the cool respite of the half-light. Will smiled and stretched out his arms and legs, then let it all flop and threw back his head. He wound in a long, expansive breath, and seemed to hold it for a moment.

"Now *that*," he said in a gush, "is what I call *being*."

"Then what do you call *this*?" Kay asked, almost as a reflex, without consideration.

Will sat up, his eyes bright and alert. "This?" He gestured around at the vines, the shadowy beams of wood and the cool brick walls. "This is actual life." With an arch flick of his eyebrows and the grin that had become, since their arrival, his new feature, he slumped back onto the bench and pulled his hood over his head, and then further over his face, while he began to hum contentedly. "This is life, life, life," he said again after a few bars.

Beyond the arbor, over the heads of hundreds of moving wraiths, Kay could still make out the elevated platform, covered by a sort of arched stone roof surmounted by a steeple, from which the single wraith seemed to be conducting the action of the garden as if, somehow, he controlled it. She watched him for a few moments while Will breathed deeply, inhaling the warm, social air around him. He was jittery, exhilarated, sharp. All of a sudden, Kay thought, he was behaving out of character. She almost didn't trust him. She almost felt abandoned. All around them, in the heavy, wet, cool air, the grapevines coursed up and down the trellises, climbing, hanging, reaching, performing delicate but muscular acts of balance and poise. Kay followed them through the shadow, picking out their interlaced strands and drawing with her eyes the routes from root to fruit again and again, as far as she could see. She braced herself.

"I thought we came here because we were going to try to find my father. Really *find him*. You said Razzio had a huge plotting board, the biggest in the world, with wraiths moving instead of stones, and acres of grapevines . . ." Kay's voice trailed off as she suddenly realized where she was. She looked around, then down, expecting to see the lines of the board under her feet, there, in the arbor where they sat. "Here," she said, "and out there, and all those wraiths out there, all of them—"

"Moving on the board!" Will said chirpily.

"But where are the lines?" Kay asked, almost of herself.

"Oh, they're all around you," Will answered, again chirpily, from beneath his hood. "But they're very small, and you have to know what you're looking for. Every blade of grass is part of the line, every pebble, every brick—and don't think Razzio's board is flat—no, it runs in every direction. In Razzio's garden, even time is laid on the grid, and every second is part of the line. To understand it, even to glimpse how you might under-stand it, you have to think of yourself as a spider that spins webs out of choices and hangs them between this, and this." He held up his right hand, his index finger jammed against his thumb. "But Razzio has the keenest eyes in the world, and he can't be outplotted." Will sighed happily, and Kay almost thought he might start humming again. "Which is why it's so relaxing being here," he added after a moment. "One doesn't bother even *trying*."

Kay thought for a minute, hard. "So you mean," she asked, "that we're on the board right now? And so our movements, and even the time we take to make them, mean something to Razzio?"

So you mean I'm some kind of pawn on a huge chessboard? That Razzio is playing me?

"Yes."

"But how can that be?" She frowned. "How can he know what we mean when we don't know ourselves?"

Will sat bolt upright, his eyes so wild that Kay regretted her question.

"That's just it," he said merrily, spookily. "That's just it.

How else could he know what we meant, except at the moment when we least knew ourselves? Oh, I hadn't realized I was so *tired!*" he said, and settled back into his hooded slouch.

Kay waited another minute as she wondered what Will would do. It was a long, quiet minute, made all the more painfully silent for the pulsing crescendos of voices, music and what sounded like footsteps that lapped like the ocean's waves against the shore of the arbor. Will slumped motionless but for the steady rise and fall of his chest.

"So you're not going to help me do this? You're not going to help me find Razzio?" *How will I find them? How will I get home?* Kay felt herself growing frustrated, and increasingly more worried with each passing second.

"Find him?" Will objected abruptly. "We've already found him. He's the one who let you in. Or, I should say, the one who put you on the board."

"You mean that butler person is Razzio?"

Will whinnied. "The butler!"

Kay considered this for a while. She found herself slightly annoyed to have her expectations upset. "Then who is that tall man directing the orchestra?"

Will sat up, pulled back his hood and faced her squarely.

"I'm sorry, Kay. You're right. I'm not being helpful. This is Razzio's house because everything that happens here means something to him. He *owns* this place. But that's all he does. You could hardly say he *lives* in it. Maybe if he lived in it, Phantastes wouldn't hate him so much. Everyone else—all the wraiths, the ones we call the causes"—he gestured around the garden at the hundreds of moving forms—"they *live* here— like us, they're on the board. That is, everyone else but two, and they are Razzio's closest advisers. Inside, somewhere, is Oidos—she—"

"I've met her," said Kay. Her voice was flat. Will looked sharply at her, as if she had been bitten by a snake; but immediately his face softened.

"Good," he said. "Oidos dwells in the place of pure knowing. But in the place of pure being, on the platform just there"—he pointed to the place where Kay had just been watching the conductor—"that's Ontos, the other of the two modes. He's not on the board. That is, he *is*, but he's fixed. He doesn't move. I don't think he has *ever* moved from that spot. That is, he moves, but his motion is a reflection of the being that is all around him. It's not only the instruments that follow his lead; everything that exists does."

"You mean he is conducting us?"

"Yes, exactly. He's conducting us. And everyone else. And everything else. Or maybe they're all conducting him."

Kay watched Ontos spin and dip, his arms swaying in repeated arcs in a motion contrary to that of his neck. His body undulated like a wave, at the same time rippling like the sudden accelerations that pulse through a murmuration of starlings. His slow dance, rhythmic, silent, was the most beautiful she had ever seen. She could hardly speak.

"It's mesmerizing," she said.

"It is," Will agreed. "It's the purest form of plotting, a complete embodiment of everything we're doing on the board, and a reflection of it. In a way, you could say that everything Oidos knows, Ontos is. She keeps in the place of pure knowing a collection of things that record whatever you could know about the wraiths who walk on Razzio's board. But in the garden Ontos lives out that knowledge as body, as movement."

Kay thought about this for a second.

"What does that mean?"

"Take that wraith over there," said Will. He had turned, and now indicated a little knot of forms, seated rapt with attention in a tight circle around a speaker. Animated and intense, she was expounding something to them, something you could see from the movement of her eyes and the sharp, crisp rhythms of her lips was important.

"She's saying something," Will suggested.

"Something serious," Kay agreed.

"Exactly. She is saying it exactly. She means what she says. Whatever it is, she is committed to it, concentrates every part of her awareness on it. And her hearers: they, too, give it every ounce of their attention, drill down on it, seize at it. Now turn away."

Will swung his gaze back to Kay, and she hers to him.

"What do you take from that? After you look at a bright light, the burn of it will leave its image in your eye. What is left, now, in your mind's eye?"

"That concentration of hers, of all of theirs. That intensity," Kay said. "That focus."

"Now look at Ontos."

Kay turned to the turning wraith. Moments before, his body had seemed to flutter and cascade, to ripple like flight or the rolling of water beneath wind; but now his gaze seemed, rather, fixed—and, while she watched, his whole body seemed to fling wide and then to contract, like petals closing on the point of a pinbright blossom. All the concentration and focus Kay had seen on the faces of those other wraiths, as if translated into another language, as if spoken in a single character, fleeted here across the expressions of Ontos's moving body.

"He feels who we are," Will murmured. "What we're made of, where we're going, what we mean. I guess only he knows what all that meaning feels like. But I'm glad someone does."

He feels what we're made of. Where we're going.

"Can I ask him? What where I'm going feels like?" she asked, but didn't bother waiting for a response.

Will's tone was suddenly sharp, urgent, like the grinding shear of tightly screwed scissors. "Kay, you can't, it doesn't work like that—"

But Kay had already walked away.

As she approached the platform that bore the gyrating form of Ontos, his lean body reflecting so much sound, heat, light and movement, she could feel the pulse of the garden begin to rise within her own blood. Though it neither knelled nor beat like a sound, it rushed in her ears; it had no taste, but her mouth was full of it; she felt nothing but air against her skin and grass on her feet as she passed toward the dais, and yet that air seemed charged with a new pressure; and she closed her eyes against the smell and held her breath against the light, and, with what seemed like the last awareness in her consciousness, she knew that she had crossed the stretch of grass and was climbing the worn stone steps up to the platform.

After that there was nothing. She had no sense of time, no fears, no regrets. Deep in a trance, she never knew how she stepped into the center of the dais; she never saw Ontos bow to her, give way to her, withdraw from her and, retreating down the steps, take his place upon the grass; and she never felt the complex contortions through which her body moved as, for more than three hours, she danced to the causes in the garden of the House of the Two Modes, the center of their being and the mirror of their movement.

3

WAR

"**K**ay. Kay."

I am not Kay—I am not—I am—

"Kay. Wake up."

Kay opened her eyes and saw only painful light. She squeezed them shut again and noticed that she had swiveled her head violently to the side.

"Let her sleep, Will."

Phantastes. Will. What am I doing?

"She's been through an ordeal," the old imaginer said.

Kay opened her eyes again, determined to see the light.

"Hello in there," said Will. He was smiling very near her face in an encouraging way. Kay felt grass beneath her hand where it lay beside her, but her head was resting on some sort of cushion or pillow, and there was a blanket drawn close around her shoulders.

You are always with me when I'm lost.

"You gave us a fright," Will said. Kay recognized that she was lying on the ground, and that Will was lying next to her, looking into her eyes.

How long have I been asleep? How long, how long—

"How long—"

"Since last night. About nine hours. But you haven't been asleep the whole time."

"That is an understatement," said Phantastes. Kay saw that he was sitting at a large stone table a few meters away. He was watching her intently. He looked concerned.

"Do you remember anything at all from . . . before?"

At Will's words, a hole seemed to open up in the world and Kay began to fall through it. Her body lurched out of her control and her arm shot out to grab Will's—anything to hold, anything to give her purchase in this world, anything to ground her in the sunlight, on the grass.

Help me.

"It's okay," he said. He was soothing her. "I've got you. Maybe don't think too hard about it. Let it in slowly."

As if she were peering round a corner or blinking against a bright light, Kay allowed herself to glimpse in snatches what she could remember of the preceding night: the conversation with Will in the arbor, the sudden resolution to talk to Ontos, striding across the grass toward the platform, and then—which was strange, like a dream—a feeling of seeing or having seen many things at once—things that didn't so much happen in order, but because of one another. And among it all there was a strong sense of movement, of her own body turning in on itself, like a flower with petals growing and blooming not out toward the sun, but inward into the stem of herself, as if she were all the light and the bud were opening into its own middle, its own core. And round that corner like planets in a ridiculous jig spun so many perceptions that it tired and dizzied her now to try to see them—the way it hurts deep between the eyes when you try to read the signs on a station platform while the train is passing by at high speed.

"Do you remember anything?" Will asked.

With effort, Kay shook her head and sat up. "What happened?"

Will scrambled to crouch beside her, and with a strong

hand placed gently on her left shoulder, he kneaded reassurance into it.

"You occupied the place of pure being," he said. "It's as simple as that."

"It's as unprecedented as that," said Phantastes.

"What Phantastes means is, Ontos has never allowed another wraith to take his place on the platform," said Will. "To be honest, we didn't think it was possible. We didn't know what would happen. And you—we don't even know who you are, really."

In the pit of her stomach Kay felt a strange twisting of pride and nausea.

"For three hours, pretty much exactly, you moved on the platform just as Ontos might have done—but it was completely different from Ontos, too. When Ontos moves, everyone and everything moves around him as normal. He mirrors the garden, the garden mirrors him; but it's as if they were in separate worlds. When you stood up there last night—it wasn't as if they acknowledged you, not that—but every wraith in the garden, every cause, seemed to turn inward. No one spoke, no one acknowledged one another. It was as if they had all become entirely engrossed in themselves."

Will was silent. His eyes, which had been on the grass as he traced the blades with his finger, looked up at her. "Do you know why? What made you fall into a trance? What did it feel like to you? Do you remember?"

Kay breathed in deeply. She closed her eyes and let her head rock back onto her shoulders. *Nothing.* She lifted her face up to the morning sky, feeling the sun pushing bright and warm through her eyelids.

"I remember just one moment," she said. "It seemed like a long moment, like a dream. In that moment I looked into Ontos's eyes. It seemed like I was looking into deep, phosphorescing pools. And in the same moment I felt like two hundred arrows being shot from a single bow in two hundred different directions. Two hundred arrows that pierced through two hundred different people, and I was in them all, sticking in them all. It was awful."

I remember your eyes well enough.

Kay could feel tears, hot ones, starting in the inner corners of her own eyes.

"And all the arrows—every arrow drove right into the stomach, right into the navel of one of the causes. But they weren't arrows. They were shards of something like glass or mirror, and they were cords—something that tied all of us to one another—and I felt this incredible pain tearing out of me, as if everything in me were heaving to get out, as if I were going to be turned inside out, and—"

"Kay," said Will. His hand tightened on her shoulder. "You don't have to remember."

I remember your eyes well enough.

Kay stopped, and opened her eyes, and looked at Will, and at Phantastes. Beyond them, twenty meters away, the causes were milling about in the garden, waking, drifting, chatting. She saw Razzio in his waistcoat standing among them, stealing glances at the three of them at the table. He looked preoccupied and nervous.

"The worst thing about it," Kay went on, "was that, even though it was a terrible pain, a tearing pain, I wanted it. Even though I hated it. Because it wasn't just pain. It was joy, too. And they were both there, pain and joy, at war inside me."

Pushing himself toward her, Will leaned in and wrapped her in a warm hug. He swayed them from side to side in a slow pattern like a tall tree in a distant breeze.

"Will, what does it mean?"

Because his head was almost resting on her head, Kay

could feel the words in his throat, the deep vibrations that she knew were true. "You went to Ontos with that question, the question about what you are doing, what you should be doing, what your purpose feels like. You shot that question out in hundreds of different directions last night. Even I felt it. Every cause on the board turned within, as if they were all staring at themselves, as if they were all suddenly intensely curious about their own being. For a long moment, for hours, they all seemed"—he paused, and breathed—"self-aware."

"In a way," said Phantastes, "you might say you asked your question of every wraith in the garden. Every one of them mirrored it. Every one of them was tied to you."

Kay pushed Will's arms away in frustration. "And what was the answer? What did they do?"

"They slept, Kay, like you. After a while they all lay down wherever they were, and they were silent and still, as if they were dead. And they slept."

So it was all for nothing. All that pain. All that awful joy. All that pushing and all that connection. All that war for nothing.

And now the tears began to gather in Kay's eyes so fast that she had no time even to sob. Will rocked her back and forth, his side by her side not so much a comfort but a deep ground and well of sorrow from which she drew bucket after bucket of tears, drawing and pouring, pouring and again drawing, in a continual motion that felt easier than anything she had ever done in her life.

"Whatever is in you, Kay, let it out now," said Will.

"But what if there is nothing in me at all?"

"What indeed."

It was a bark like that of a dog: short, peremptory, fierce, the menace before a fight.

It came from Razzio. He stood behind the great stone table at which Phantastes was seated. From where Kay was sitting on the grass, he seemed to tower above it despite his size, and the turret of that tower was contempt. The sneer on his face seemed to bite into her eyes when she looked at him: aggressive, bitter and revolted.

"As if you were the victim," he said. "As if any of this concerned you. That you should dare even to think so." He spat on the table.

"Razzio—" Will put out one of his arms in a vain effort to plot away the old left-wraith's anger, to ward him off with the swirl of his fingers.

Razzio made a fist and held it up before his face. He stared at it as it tightened. He seemed to be striving to crush his own fingers. Kay felt everything in her body and her mind withdrawing from his awful fury—everything but her eyes, which remained fixed, nailed to that tightening fist.

He slammed it down on the stone, making a crunching sound that Kay knew was not the table giving way before skin and bone, but skin and bone compressing and breaking on the unyielding surface of the table. She expected Razzio to shout or cry out, but his face remained stubbornly impassive. He seemed more curious about his hand than pained by it. Like the rest of them, stunned and paralyzed, he stood regarding the broken tissue of his fist where it lay before him.

"This is how it should be," he said quietly as he regarded his hand—quietly, but his voice was still a thin thread of rage. "It should be like this. There are bounds. There are impassable limits. A plotter cannot plot without these securities." Behind him the causes had awoken. They now stood still and expectant throughout the garden.

Razzio drew himself up to his stout tallest. He held up his right fist then, with his left hand, finger by finger, pried it apart. It was already starting to show a bruise along the inside edge of the palm, and unfolding it seemed to take all his concentration, as if he were meditating on the pain it caused him. Kay felt Will's own hand on her shoulder as a stay against Razzio's fury. Her tears were drying on her face; she could feel them hardening, pursing together the skin of her cheeks in the fresh, cool air of the winter's morning.

Razzio stood still, regarding his hand. He looked at the table before him. With another sudden burst of energy he laid his arm on the edge of the table, then dragged it in an arc right across it. A few plates, several glasses and a candlestick, a book and some clothing fell to the ground, some of it shattering. He seemed neither to notice nor to care. Phantastes had pushed himself back to avoid the sweep of Razzio's arm; now they stared at each other.

"I am angry," said Razzio.

"We can see that," said Phantastes.

"I make no apology for my anger." Razzio took a seat opposite Phantastes, and with his left hand smoothed the creases and crumples in his clothing. "Sit at the table, all of you," he said. He did not look at them. Nor did he wait for them to take their places before he began to speak.

"I have watched your approach to the House of the Two Modes. I have watched it with growing disquiet. Ghast had no business interfering with the little girl, the author; she ought to have been brought here, where she might have found her room in the place of pure knowing. Ghast should not have attacked you in Alexandria, and the murder of our brother, Pyrexis, is a crime that will never be blotted from our story. By the stone," he said, "that pocky mank-wraith has gone too far. I may not have been a friend to the imaginers—" Here he looked pointedly at Phantastes. "Indeed, I may never be a friend to the imaginers, but even *I* can see that we must return the Society to cohesion, to unity. Had you seen what I have seen on the board many times lately, you might not even have risked coming here."

Razzio turned to Phantastes and addressed him directly. "My most ancient antagonist, we have not spoken for many centuries. You have suffered a terrible reversal of fortune, caused in no small part by my own ambition for primacy in the assembly. I do not hesitate to acknowledge my part in this. I cannot think what grief it must be to you to be robbed of your temple, to suffer daily the loss of that immortal flower that was the root of your art and function. Had I been deprived of the board, I should surely have lost my mind; though its loss is by its very nature the one chance I cannot, with any kind of plotting, forecast. Indeed, this single blind spot in my art has for many years been the subject of my most intense speculation." Here he turned, and focused eyes of such deep and penetrating incision on Kay that she almost squirmed beneath them. "I think you know how Ghast conspired to dissolve the Society of Wraiths and Phantasms and to lead the wraiths out of Bithynia into exile. You may have learned something of my own regrettable part in the swelling of this ulcerous boil that now grows to such a head and crust. But there is one thing you cannot know, one thing that all the stories in the world cannot narrate, that even the dreams of the last imaginer of the timeless temple of Alexandria cannot picture, because even I myself could not see it, and still cannot. All I can see is that it has a great deal to do with you, our new young friend."

Razzio closed his eyes and folded his hands across his stomach. Kay, by contrast, sat up in her chair, her eyes glistening like those of a cat on the hunt.

"I must tell you what has happened here. I am not a great storyteller. You must bear with me."

Kay saw the quick glance Will shot Phantastes, but Phantastes, with his eyes closed, took no notice.

"The plots have always changed for as long as the board has been," began Razzio. "The wraiths drift and dance about the garden, Ontos conducts them, and I gather up from him, from them and from the places of pure knowing, an estimation of things. This estimation is never the same, because the world beyond the board is constantly changing. Sometimes Ontos dances intricately and with the most minute articulations of fingers and eyes; then I must spend hours roaming through the rooms of pure knowing, and Oidos opens a thousand drawers before I can resolve the plot, which is long, difficult and involved. Sometimes, by contrast, the wraiths in the garden slouch and are silent, and Ontos hardly moves at all; then I sit with Oidos on one of the great thrones, and we watch the light drift by for hours across the bare walls of a stately room. On other days I must run—I do, I must run—through the places of pure knowing, frantically searching for the signs that will connect and interpret the motions of the wraiths in the garden. Once I sat for a week with a piece of blank paper in my hand, while all the while Ontos slept. But even then a plot emerged from the causes, the dance of forms, the places of pure knowing; a plot *always* emerges.

"Two months ago this changed. I was walking through the garden in the morning, as I always do, taking note of the positions of each of the wraiths—every one of them a cause that plots an entity on the board. You know roughly how it works: instead of stones on a board I read people and things in the garden, setting them in play and then watching their movements day by day. All the things interact in some way with Ontos, even if only by ignoring him and his conducting; and from observing him I can also judge the mode of the movement—is it happy? Sad? Optimistic? Made in fear? In love? Then I know what the movement is, and its mood. I take this in to Oidos, I place the fact and the mode, by certain clues collected in the garden, against one or more of the ten thousand things she preserves in the place of pure knowing. From the union of movement, mood and knowledge, understanding arises; and these understandings present themselves as narratives. Century after century I have studied Ontos in the evening, walked the garden in the morning and spent the afternoon in the house of the ten thousand things. Always the day yields up its journey. Always I take to my bed its insight.

"But two months ago, while walking in the garden, I observed something strange. On the grass near the dais one of the causes lay asleep. This in itself was not unusual—many wraiths sleep in the garden. Some sleep *only* in the garden. But this wraith was sleeping at a time when Ontos himself was writhing with acrobatic intensity. Every other wraith in the garden was surging with unbounded energy. Nor did this wraith awake the day after, or the day after that. Indeed, it was not *just* a sleep, but something deeper. And since that day, another twenty-three causes have, without obvious explanation, slipped into the same coma. Each time I have watched them. Each time I have removed them to a prepared infirmary inside. Each time I have tended them carefully, trying to keep them alive. If one should die—what would that mean for the board? How could I understand the *disappearance of a cause?*"

While Razzio was speaking, one of the causes had put fruit on the table. Will had a grape between the fingers of his right hand. Again and again he was raising it a few centimeters above his plate; again and again he was dropping it. Kay stared at the grape while Razzio gathered his thoughts.

"You must understand the importance of this event. I cannot finish my plotting without the causes. Instead of reaching an understanding, I am left in ignorance. This is quite unprecedented, quite unlike anything that has ever happened before."

His eyes still closed and his hands still folded loosely across his stomach, Razzio reclined in silence in his chair. The other two wraiths said nothing. Kay looked back and forth from one face to the other, but both Phantastes and Will were blank. She sat up and put her hands on the table. She wanted answers.

"Where are these causes going? And why does it matter if—" She stopped, realizing that what she had been about to say would probably offend Razzio. "I mean, what will happen if you can't plot?"

What does any of this have to do with me?

No one answered.

The three wraiths sat in complete stillness, just as they had before. Nothing happened. Kay reached forward and took some grapes; one by one she plucked them off, put them in her mouth, chewed them and swallowed them. She put her hands in her lap. She put her hands on the edge of the chair behind her back. It was no use. Every moment passed like a sentence beginning with the same word and, no matter what she did, the moment ended and began again, and ended and began again, the same. She didn't notice the tension in her arms and legs until she was almost ready to scream.

"You know what this means," said Will softly when he finally did speak.

"The end of beauty," Phantastes whispered.

Kay slammed a flat palm down on the stone table. It hardly made a sound. She didn't raise her head, but she knew that they were all looking at her, and that they all knew exactly what she wanted. Will pushed back his chair, and Kay could sense out of the corner of her eye that he was carefully turning to face her. As she waited for him, she noticed that, where her hand had curled on the table, her knuckles had turned white.

I've seen that before. I make no apology for my anger.

"Plotters work with boards, Kay," he said. "The boards are of a certain size. We move the stones around the boards, watching the patterns. Our hands think through the narratives of things as they guide and are guided by the stones. But always the stones stay on the board and the narratives are, as we say, conserved. If stones could fall off the board or come onto the board from nowhere, the plotting would cease to function properly. For that reason, there is nothing a plotter fears more than the edge of the board; nothing a plotter guards more carefully than the security of the stones. Causes must generate effects, and effects derive from causes; a cause without an effect or an effect without a cause would break the principle of conservation, and would undermine the plot.

"The greatest stories flirt with the edge, and become great

exactly because of this flirtation. They skirt it, needle it, always toying with the loss of a cause or with the spontaneous effect; but the art of the greatest storytellers lies in the surprise of conservation, in the delight of an expectation dashed, only to be fulfilled. It may be a simple rule, but it is a rule nonetheless.

"One of our most ancient stories is that of return. A man goes away, then comes back. At home perhaps he leaves a wife and a child. Think that this man goes off to war, and that the war eats up ten years of his life. Imagine that his journey home is thwarted. Call him Odysseus, king of Ithaka. Imagine his wife, Penelope, sitting beside their bed every night of those ten years, then another ten, expecting his return. Down the stairs, through two or three strong stone-framed doors, see her child, Telemachus, being carried out of the hall by his nurse. Penelope is followed from the room by the taunts and jeers of a hundred drunken and dangerous men, her suitors—no better than vultures circling in the absence of her husband, the king, men aspiring to seize his throne, men spending the wealth of Odysseus's royal house. They are impatient. See the snarling and the sharp-toothed smiles behind their grimy beards, when they demand of Penelope every morning, *How long—how long must we wait for your decision? How long until you forget the return of your husband, until you give up your expectation that he will return?* She despairs. By night she lies undreaming and rigid in her bed, wishing that, should she fall asleep, this Odysseus, this man—the cause of all this—would return by morning, would deliver her from her despair. She develops a ruse to ward off the impatience of her suitors: she weaves a shroud for her husband's father and promises the suitors that she will choose one among them to be her new husband, that she will forget Odysseus, once the shroud has been completed. By day she weaves this shroud, the symbol of her forgetting; by night, in place of her anxious despair, she unravels the threads, remembering her husband, cleaving fast to her love for him. Ravel, unravel, ravel, unravel; forget, recall, forget, recall. Meanwhile, on the sea, Odysseus is making for home. Always beyond the shore of Ithaka, though he may come to a stall, he never comes to a stop. She may weave and weave; but always she recalls. The edge between forgetting and recalling, between weaving and unraveling, becomes a habit for Penelope; for landlorn Odysseus the edge between hurry and delay becomes a habit, too, and, in the long years of his wandering, his nature. The story begins to look as if it will go on forever, and there is a night, as Penelope cries herself to sleep, when she recognizes her own comfort with the edge as despair. She lies along it all night like a knife."

Kay found herself holding her temples hard, with her eyes squeezed shut. Will's voice had become so aggressive, so fast. He was so angry. She could understand his anger, the anger in his words, even if she did not understand the words. She was thinking instead of her mother: alone, frightened, anxious, lying awake in the night, waiting for their return. "Make the story end," she cried weakly. "That's all I want. Make it end."

Razzio stood up abruptly, pushing his chair back violently across the cobbles. "Oh, but it *has* ended, child," he said. His voice was suddenly as stern as iron once more. "It ended yesterday when you climbed onto the dais and all twenty-four wraiths woke from their slumbers at a stroke. In a single instant they opened their eyes. In a single motion they rose from their beds and filed into the garden. Behold them now," he said, gesturing with his bruised hand in a wide arc around him. Looking up, Kay realized with a shock that the twenty-four wraiths had quietly and without ceremony circled the table, and now stood watching them. Their faces were entirely blank. "I *demand* an explanation," said Razzio.

Kay was stunned. They all were.

"But there is no explanation that you can give me, because this is not your story. You know as little about it as you know about yourself and, by the stone, that's little enough. This is not your story; it is my story. It is my story, and I will no longer sit idly by and watch Ghast presume to meddle with it.

"I have been working here in my garden for several years on a particular project. It is a great endeavor, the most difficult task I have ever set myself. There are many kinds of story, as we all know. We know their sources, their characteristics. We know how to evolve them. In the Weave, at the Feast of the Twelve Nights, together we composed stories of many kinds—dream visions, great epics, tales of love and friendship, quests, myths, great landscapes of exploration and conquest, stories of battles, of self-discovery, stories of perseverance, hope and survival, stories of despair, loss and defeat. But the methods by which we made our stories were imperfect, and even if they resulted in a great profusion of stories, they never resulted in perfect ones. As long as I have been in the Honorable Society, we have never told the *perfect* story. Always there was room for improvement. Always there was a need to keep going.

"For the last several years I have been toiling almost without rest to create the most perfect stories that can be, one of every type: a story of love, a story of conquest, a story of discovery and so on. I have set in motion among the causes ideas and actions of such beauty and precision that their every least quirk and oddity has been a revelation. We have discovered and made much in this time. In the last few months I have neared the completion of my goal. To Ghast I sent the fruits of my labors, for we had a bargain. From him I expected advancement—I do not shame to say it. In return for these blueprints, the instruction manual for building the greatest stories ever to be told, he promised that I should be elevated, that I should be made first among the twelve knights. We have not held a Weave in many years, but now we shall never require one again; I have created a method for composing stories better than any such quarrelsome, noisy congregation could produce."

Beside her, Will had turned white as a sheet.

"But Ghast did not honor his bargain with me," said Razzio. "I sent my writings to the mountain, where I understood he was testing them. This was not my concern. But he did not respect them. He hired *editors*. They *changed* my stories. The jewels I had cut were hammered and smashed. The fine details of my brushwork were scrubbed down and washed away. In that rank and rat-infested rubbish tip he calls the

Bindery, these editors dragged thick pens across my genius—for *money*! And to crown his betrayal, having sold my life's work to hucksters for nothing but dirty coin, Ghast, a *clerk*—that squat dwarf with more warts than words—presumed to launch his barge for Bithynia."

Razzio was now standing before the table, his hands splayed on its surface in a way that, given the purple bruise seeping up toward his wrist, made Kay wince.

"*For Bithynia.* Let him play the Sergeant in the mountain, and unseat the old ways. I do not much care, so long as he leaves me master of my own art. But Ghast will not be *my* king in Bithynia. I will not see the mysteries of my art cut into scraps and greased for loose change by a pack of scavenging jackals. This is a war, and I will win it."

Kay glanced at the twenty-four wraiths that surrounded them. They seemed suddenly menacing, too close, their eyes too blank, the hands at their sides too strong. Beyond them the other causes stood equally immobile and expectant, all eyes—hundreds of eyes—turned toward Razzio. Everyone in the garden except for the three of them—Will, Phantastes and Kay herself—appeared to be *ready* for something.

"What will you do?" Kay asked.

"I will leave the House of the Two Modes for the mountain," said Razzio. He said it directly to her. "Ontos, Oidos and all the causes will go with me. We will occupy the mountain, possess it and fortify it. I do not doubt that the plotters will swarm to us. And when the imaginers see that I oppose Ghast, well, they will choose any alternative to his ignorant brutality."

Kay's mind stuttered and whirled.

But you were supposed to help me. *They promised that you would help* me. *Ell. Dad. To go home. My* home.

"You were supposed to help me," she said. "I came here so that you could help me."

"But this was never your story," Razzio told her. "It is *my* story. Overnight I issued my instructions. In a few hours the causes will ready a hundred balloons, and we will launch from the garden at dawn tomorrow. You are welcome to return to the mountain with us," he said to Will and Phantastes.

He looked at Kay. His eyes bored into her heart. "You are not. Your story—your father's story—it is a distraction."

Will stood up. "Razzio—"

He hardly needed to make a gesture. Four of the causes stepped forward, two taking up places on either side of Will, and two on either side of Phantastes. Kay sprang out of her chair like a startled cat, expecting to feel hands around her arms, expecting to be lifted or bound. But no one touched her.

"As I say, the First Wraith and the last of the imaginers are both welcome to return with us to the mountain," said Razzio. "So welcome that I think I must insist."

Kay ran. Folding her body low, she threw herself like a rock between the legs of the causes that blocked her way, spinning through their arms, then tearing past the scattered clumps of wraiths who seemed—but too late, arm after arm—to think they should stop her. She ran for the doors, for any door, any way of slipping into the place of pure knowing.

Oidos said she would show me my place. "When you are ready, return, and I will help you. You, too, have a room in the place of pure knowing."

Dodging benches, shrubs and water, half flying across the cobbles and the grass, and at last sprinting round the piles of sailcloth and instruments that Razzio's minions had begun to pile by the garden walls, she flew at the nearest of the great glass doors. She turned the handle, with a huge heave forced it open, and crushed herself through the tiny gap. From room to room she sprinted, through door after door, her only thought to lay down as much distance and confusion behind her as she possibly could.

You lied to me. All of you. No one ever meant to help me at all. You all only ever think about yourselves.

Liars. Liars.

As she ran, the great empty rooms seemed to hold the sound of her cries, even long after she was gone.

4

THE TOMB

After much exertion, Kay had finally come to rest on a little bed in an attic room, squeezed in under the eaves in a tight wedge where the bed's end met the sloping ceiling. Here she crouched, listening—listening for the sound of a footfall, for the sound of voices, for the sound of any human noise. She longed to be rescued, but also felt sure that she would either cower or run if she heard someone coming. Outside, the sky had slid from gray midday into a long and increasingly murky afternoon, and from her corner, she now grew anxious at the onset of night.

What if I want to go back? How will I find my way back in the dark?

She thought of the narrow, circular stairwell up which

she had raced, taking two stone steps at a time until her thighs burned with the effort. She hadn't seen any lights on the stairs, nor did there appear to be a switch or a bulb anywhere in this room. On one side an attic window looked out across the green lawns by which they had approached the day before; standing opposite, another attic window surveyed the garden below. Kay had resisted the urge to look out of this window.

She watched the vague light drift, wondering which of the wraiths called this shabby, dim room home. Apart from the single bed that stood in its corner, all it contained was a long, low table at its very center on which were laid seventeen large, sharp, fixed-blade knives and a long coil of heavy pitched rope.

From her pocket Kay retrieved the little red book, and read again and again the passage written in her father's hand. She felt she was looking for something.

When at last she heard footsteps approaching up the stairs several doors down the corridor, she wasn't sure what her nerves were telling her. Maybe it was Will or Phantastes—the tread was light but careful, as of someone looking about him. But maybe it was one of the causes, sent to comb the place of pure knowing until they found and retrieved her. Kay thought about hiding under the bed. With a knife. Or she pictured herself running.

Instead, she sat up. Oidos stopped at the door, looking at her. Gaunt but strong, her regal figure seemed to occupy the whole frame.

"You have met Katalepsis, I think," she said. "Strange that, of all the rooms, you should choose hers. And this is only hers. No other wraith or phantasm comes here."

"One of the knives is missing," said Kay, pointing to the table where there was a gap.

"Yes," said Oidos. "I noticed it was gone almost at once, last time she was here. That was several years ago. I suppose she wanted me to be prepared. Perhaps she wanted to apologize. As I told you yesterday, Rex's death was only the distant thunder made by a stroke long past."

Kay pulled up her knees and put her arms around them.

"Ask me for the answer you most desire," said Oidos. "I will tell you."

"You told me," said Kay, "that I, too, had a room in the place of pure knowing. Take me there."

"Yes, child. But I cannot promise that you will like what you find. Follow me."

Oidos moved with deliberate evenness across the room and out through the far door. Torn between fear and curiosity, Kay didn't at first get up. Instead she waited, listening to the wraith's tread pass on and almost out of hearing.

Kay knew that this was her chance, her opportunity to learn what she meant in this place, what this place meant to her. But. *I cannot promise that you will like what you find.* Far in the distance, Oidos was almost gone.

Kay leaped to the floor, jammed the red book back in her pocket and sprinted after her. From room to room she raced, and round one of the corners. Oidos was waiting at the stairwell door.

"We haven't got much time before the light fails completely," said the old wraith. Kay knew it was a reproach for her dawdling. "My footing is not what it was. You go first."

Kay stepped before Oidos into the stairwell and started down. Much of the descent they took in complete darkness; only occasionally did an open door throw a luminous square of light upon the gray stone slabs. Down the center of the circular staircase a vertical column of stone dropped; the steps followed round in a tight ring, the walls seeming to close ever nearer upon them as they went deeper and deeper into the building. Kay thought she counted three floors, but still they climbed down. The air began to feel wet upon her skin, and the darkness hung impenetrable between her hands and face.

"You noticed yesterday," said Oidos from above her as they trudged slowly down, "that something was missing from Rex's room, didn't you?"

Kay said that she had.

"Sometimes," said Oidos, "I move things in the place of pure knowing. I have my reasons. It is here, child. There is a sill and a door. Turn to the right and you will find an iron ring."

Kay felt for the huge iron ring—as wide and heavy as a shackle. She grasped it in both hands and turned it, and the solid door creaked off its latch. Oidos leaned over her and pushed it open with a strong arm, her foot braced on the step behind. The air beyond was as cold as earth, and smelled musty.

"Sometimes I move things. And sometimes, very occasionally, I find it necessary to forget things. There should be a lantern on the other side of the room, child."

Kay had stepped down off the stone sill into the dark room. She had no idea how large it was, but she could sense the ceiling low above her, and the sound of Oidos's voice seemed to hit near walls, and be absorbed by them. She felt before her face for a table, for a lantern.

What am I, then? What does my room contain? It contains a lantern.

"This is where I bring things that I want to forget," said Oidos. Kay spun round so fast that she lost her balance. She was falling as she heard the door move. "I am sorry, child, but now I must forget you."

The heavy door swung on its hinges, and its latch dropped into place. Kay was on the earthen floor. She could feel dirt under her fingers. And try as she might, that was all that she could feel.

There is no room for me after all. Liars.

Kay crawled over, and ran her hands up and down the broad oak. There was no handle on this side.

Down on her knees again, Kay turned so that her back was against the door. In the utter darkness she pushed off onto her hands and knees and crawled slowly across the floor.

She said there was a lantern. Let there be a lantern.

After a few minutes of tentative shifting on the damp, gritty surface of the floor, she crushed the tips of her fingers against a stone wall. It had texture, ridges running across it, up it, in arcs and lines. As her hands explored its carved patterns, she tried—and failed—to visualize it. Slowly she rose to her feet, terrified that she might hit something with her head, all the time following the wall with her hands, sweeping them in ever greater circles, taking in the rich pattern and flow of the worked stone.

And then her hands hit a ledge. On the ledge was a lantern. Beside it lay a box of matches.

On her third attempt Kay struck a match. It lasted long enough for her to see the wick of the oil lamp inside a glass dome. In the darkness she removed the glass and set it down. She struggled with the matches, managed to light another, and somehow fumbled the lantern alight. She found that it stood in a little niche carved into the rock wall. She lifted the lantern by its handle and turned round.

She was not in a room at all. Before her, about three meters away, was the oak door through which she had come. It had been shut firmly behind her, and now made a perfect seal with the stone. Kay knew it was pointless to worry at it, pointless to pound on it, pointless to think any further about it. Oidos had forgotten her. Kay turned to the left.

Before her, as far as her eye could see, stretched a narrow passage. It seemed to slope slightly downward, but otherwise ran perfectly straight. The walls that bounded it to either side had been roughly carved with geometrical patterns, much like those she had seen the day before on the walls of the place of pure knowing. These carvings started just above the floor and reached well over Kay's head; above them, the passage arched roughly, little more than a hewn tunnel. For the moment Kay avoided thinking about the carvings; first she wanted to know where the passage led. The blood was pounding in her temples and neck. She held the lantern before her face and began to walk.

After about twenty paces she noticed a little recessed alcove on the right. It had been roughly bricked up, using pale, heavy square stones and thick globs of mortar. Kay pushed at the bricks, but they were firm. She kept walking. She passed four more alcoves of the same kind, two to either side, all four bricked up in the same way. Now she could see an end to the passage ahead, where a simple, roughly chiseled wall, all gray stone and dirt, faced her. It was slick with moisture, and as she approached it she began to smell soft earth, the stench of decay. She almost turned back.

Now what? Let her forget. Fine. Let her lose me in this dead abyss of tunnels. Let Razzio forget his loyalty to Ghast, his love for his own board. Let Will forget that he promised me my father, my sister, my home. Let them all forget.

But I won't forget. I choose to remember. I am Katharine Worth-More, and I am not giving up.

She hardened herself against the stench, and kept going. As she drew closer, she found that the wall was not the tunnel's end but a corner; turning left, she found the ruins of another doorway, this one framed all in stone; hanging to one side on rusted iron hinges, rotten hunks of wood were all that was left of the once-thick door. As Kay picked her way through the gap, something about the smell of the rot touched her with fear, and in the close quiet of the tunnel she suddenly had the sensation that she wasn't alone. Spinning round, she knocked the lantern against the door frame, cracking the glass. The flame sputtered, but kept burning.

"Hello?" Kay threw her voice beyond the near glow of the light, back round the corner, hoping to hear . . . *what?*

Hoping to hear wraiths scraping their knees on roof tiles.

She took a deep breath. Bringing the lantern close to her chest this time, feeling its heat warm and comfortable on her shirt, she turned back to the only way forward.

No sooner had she done so than she gasped in shock. Her stomach rose into her mouth, and she nearly dropped the lantern. This passage, like the other, was marked at intervals with bricked-up alcoves. But around them, both walls, all of white marble almost from floor to ceiling, had been deeply carved in exact relief with incredible intricacy—and the scenes were so lifelike in their animated, flowing shapes that she thought the forms, like straining gargoyles, might rip shrieking out of their stillness into live motion. On one side—her left—human figures processed down the passage, leading animals and, further on, other people bound in chains toward a distant altar. Kay paced down the straight passage, taking it all in, holding the lamp high to catch the full sweep of it: the gravity and seriousness of the cloaked figures, and the terror and anger of the captives and beasts; the columns of people, the swaying trees, the distant hills; and everywhere she looked, no children, no laughter, no lovers, no sign of speech. Notwithstanding the hard, dull grain of the stone, when she peered closely at any one of the shackled faces, she could see the passion cut with minute detail, as if the walls were not walls but the shrunken and petrified remains of a real procession, of real priests and their sacrificial victims. At the end of the passage the carved scenes culminated in a massive altar, stone within stone, supporting the weight of a grim-faced, limb-stiff victim lying sprawled across its surface, awaiting the knife. But then Kay

saw something else, as if the stone image before her had flickered, or her eyes had changed depth—and suddenly it was not
a victim splayed on an altar but Ontos lolling on his dais, so
lifelike that she half expected the form to turn and stare at her.
Below him the altar itself, the dais, began to turn and whorl
so that it lifted off its base like a great stone flower, and in the
unsteady lamplight seemed almost to rise continuously before
her eyes.

With a sick heave of her gut, Kay thought of the hours she
had spent on that platform the night before. *I lay on that altar.
I am going to die here. I am going to die.* She reeled, feeling sick,
with Phantastes's skeptical warning pounding in her ears—*An
open hand can be trusted.* But his eyes were saying, *Don't trust
them, Kay; Kay, don't give your heart to a closed fist.* As her
head swam, she found herself leaning against the rock at the
far end of the passage, breathing hard. Beads of sweat stood
out on her forehead, and her body hung from her hands where
they gripped the stone. *Why? Why of all the places in the world
am I here?* Her mind staggered across the events of the last few
days—the balloon, the Quarries, Alexandria, Naxos, Rome—
with all the faces and questions, the anger of Ghast, Flip's
gentle steel, Will and his childlike, openhanded yearning, the

library, the tree of Byblos, Rex's blood silent on stone. And never, no matter where they went, no matter what they did, no matter whom they met, they never seemed to be one step closer to Ell, or their father, never one step closer to their mother's lonely tears. *Not even on Naxos, staring out to sea, Rex dead at my feet, did I feel so alone. This has all been for nothing. Nothing at all.*

She stared down between her hands. With a start she realized that she had set the lantern on the floor and was leaning on an altar, a real altar, her hands upon the place of sacrifice, dyed with the blood of how many victims she could not imagine. She would have torn her hands away in revulsion had she not been paralyzed, turned to very stone herself. Her heart began to spasm, chiseling in her chest with heavy, blunt force.

How many victims—how many times—and I am the last—and this is my tomb—

Like the crack that breaks the dam, that little word released a torrent of recognitions. For suddenly Kay saw that this passage *was* a tomb, and an ancient one, built to the same pattern as the passage tombs to which their father had dragged them, all over Ireland, a few summers before. Low-ceilinged, long, carved—and at what must be the western end, the altar. *Mum.*

What nightmare is this? Kay swayed there, shaking for a long while, squeezing her eyes shut against the tears. At her feet the discarded lamp sputtered again, but again did not quite go out.

When at last she opened her dark eyes, she was almost surprised to find everything still the same. The passage narrowed toward the western end, closing round the back of the altar, and as her vision cleared, she found she was barely inches from the north wall—this one immediately different from the one along which she had earlier crawled in fear. The first thing she noticed was that here the lines were softer, and not so acutely chiseled into the stone. As her head cleared, she stepped back, picked up the lamp and began to take in this other scene. The figures it showed were all leaving the temple now, the empty altar behind them free of blood, the heavy cloaks and shackles thrown away somewhere out of sight. With every pace back toward the door, the faces cheered and grew merrier: first the brows lifted and the cheeks bulged and dimpled, then the ears lay back and the corners of the mouths turned up, then the eyes seemed to sparkle and the nostrils flared above rows of gappy white teeth—teeth that caught sparks of mica in the stone and seemed in the lamplight to flash with joy. Hands were joined and raised in the air, arms clapped backs, and one group even formed a ring, circling feverishly as they dunked one of their number with jocund mercilessness in a vat of half-pressed grapes. With a start Kay recognized the long hair and elegant, boned knuckles that gripped the edge of the vat as those of Oidos.

Conservation. Of course. The sacrifice complete, the wraiths save themselves, and return to their festive humor. It was all leading up to this. It was all leading up to this, for me, and this is nothing. No Dad, no Mum, no Eloise. And now, no Kay.

Kay thought that she had never been truly at the end until now. Of course the others would look for her. Of course they would go to Oidos and to Razzio and press them for answers. But Kay knew how rigid and silent those two wraiths could be; getting answers from them would take time. Kay had always made promises to herself. Her promises generally took a negative form: *I will never . . . I will not . . .*

This time, she thought, *it will be different.*

Kay made a promise to herself. *If I get out of this place, if I can just get away, I will go home. I promise myself that I will go home, and I will take my family with me. Nothing will stop me.*

She sat heavily on the floor, sliding down against the wall, scraping what felt like chunks from the skin over her spine.

Her lantern began to flicker. Kay was looking at it and

tapping the tank at its base when one of the square stones in the alcove in front of her began to move.

She didn't notice getting to her feet. She noticed being on them, crouching, holding the wall. She noticed the sweat that stood suddenly on her hairline. She noticed the light flickering, and she willed it to be steady, willed it to last.

And she noticed the stone, edging slowly forward, a meter away. She drew a pace closer.

With sudden force, the stone lurched forward out of the wall and crunched to the ground beneath. It toppled over, one of its squared corners hitting the carving on the far side of the passage, chipping it. Kay took no notice. She was staring at the black hole left in the bricked wall of the alcove, through which the head of an iron staff had—only for a moment—protruded.

An iron staff topped by a snake writhing to the hilt of a sword.

I've seen that before.

And then the lantern gave out. In the heavy cloth of dark that she now stood in, Kay began to shout in inarticulate syllables. It felt as if the dark were forcing its way into her mouth, stifling her attempts to form words. She was terrified, drowning in dark. Her lungs tore at the air, both trying and failing to take it in. After a few seconds, still panting, she clawed at the stone wall, cramming her face against the stones, trying to listen. There was nothing. She screamed again, this time calling out for help, calling out for rescue. Again she listened, and again she heard only her own breath until that, too, faded, leaving her with nothing but the faint noise of her own skin, her own ears.

And then, there was just silence.

Why would you do that? Why would you leave me? Who would do such a thing?

In the dark Kay reached for the fallen stone. With both hands she hefted it into her lap where she sat in the void, her back to the stone wall, and cradled it as if it were her child and she its mother.

Hours might have passed. Kay's body grew cold, her joints stiff. Her fingers where she gripped the heavy stone and her leg where its weight pressed into her flesh had long since become numb. She hadn't cried; her cheeks were as dry as her throat. She felt neither hunger nor thirst. She felt nothing so acute as loneliness. All she knew, as the time of emptiness fell on her like a shadow in the night, was her own awareness of a slow loss of sensation.

Eloise. Mum. Dad. Eloise. Mum. Dad. Eloise. Mum. Dad.

The names circled in her head with a rhythm that had become her only time, her only space, her only sensation. She had heard—as most do—that your life passes before your eyes at the moment of your death. *It's not true*, she thought. *The names pass over your tongue.*

Soon all other thoughts vanished until only the names were left. *Eloise. Mum. Dad.*

She didn't notice the footsteps when they first approached. She hadn't been listening for them. She hadn't been listening for anything. It was only after they had come and were drawing away again that she suddenly realized—like a body startled out of death—what she had very nearly missed.

The footsteps were passing on the other side of the wall.

Frantic, she scrabbled to her feet, turned and put her face to the aperture, screaming all the while for help, for rescue, for anything, for those feet to return.

She screamed so loudly and for so long that she couldn't hear the voice answering her from beyond the wall. Her wildly working mouth had forced her eyes shut, or she might have seen the glow of another lantern, and might have seen, too— rather than felt—the hand reaching toward her through the gap in the wall.

"Kay," said the hand. It hadn't tried to grab her. Its flat palm—firm, facing downward—had called for silence. "Kay, stand back."

She stood back. After a few seconds something very hard hit the stones from behind. Then it hit them again, and again. They shook. And again. The mortar between them started to shake loose, and then the stones seemed to buckle. A bulge formed in the wall as, kick upon kick, it started to give way. At last, with a crunching and a crumpling sound, the whole wall tumbled into a heap in the passage before her. Light pooled against the white walls of the passage.

After a few more seconds, a long leg swung out through the gap. Kay rushed to the opening. Attached to the leg was Flip.

And then, at long last, the sobs came.

5

SACRIFICE

Flip allowed Kay to cry for a few minutes. They sat beside each other on the pile of stones, Flip holding one of her hands with both of his, as if he were holding a butterfly or a breath of air. Kay knew he was eager to get away, to climb back through the hole in the wall—but he said nothing at all, only looked at her hand and, when she sobbed, raised his eyebrows at each gasp, as if to acknowledge, as if to honor it.

"Kay," he said when her sobs had run out, "we need to go."

As they climbed back through the rubble of the broken wall, Flip carefully guiding Kay's steps over the loose stones, he tried to explain what had happened to him on that day on Naxos: how he had sat by the sea through the day and night, soaked and shivering, anguished by Phantastes's accusation, worried about Will's safety; how he had walked along the causeway to the little island in the harbor, to stand on the spot where Rex had died; how he had loitered there, looking at the stone ground without a thought in his head, until by the first light of day he had noticed something curious.

"With his blood, Kay, Rex had written on the stones. He must have used his finger. Maybe it was the last thing he ever did. The writing wasn't neat, but it was unmistakable. I stared at it for hours, trying to decipher what it meant."

No. He couldn't have.

"Flip, I was with him—in my hands—his head in my hands when—" She stopped.

"He must have, Kay. No one else could have written it."

Flip held up his lantern. They had begun walking again, very slowly down a low, narrow passage. This tunnel had nothing like the ample proportions of the other, nor did it show any decoration at all. Flip nearly had to crouch in order to protect his head and shoulders from the rough rock above. But Kay noticed that he was watching the floor of the passage all the time, studying it as they passed.

"What did it say?"

"He wrote a word in Greek. *Taphoi*. It's what we call this place."

"The House of the Two Modes?"

"No. These tunnels. The catacombs. The place of burial."

"Why do you call them that?"

Flip stopped before one of the alcoves, and pressed his fingers along the grooves between the mortared stones. Now he looked at her sharply. "Don't you know what this place is?"

Kay just looked back at him. Without another word, Flip passed her the lantern and crouched on the tunnel floor. In the sand and powder of the passage he drew a square with his finger, and then, through it, a cross, bisecting the sides of the square at their midpoints. Around the square he drew a circle; its circumference touched the corners of the square and the ends of the cross, binding the whole.

"The square is the House of the Two Modes," said Kay.

"Yes," said Flip. He looked up. "And beneath it are the catacombs: two passages at right angles running under the garden, and a huge ring around the whole structure. The catacombs, containing the tombs of the members of the Honorable Society. When wraiths and phantasms die, when they are killed, this is where we bury them."

Kay almost dropped the lantern. Instead she held it with both hands. It shook. Every tiny hair on her body felt like a worm, and the worms were crawling all over her.

"Can you die?"

Flip put his hand on Kay's elbow as if to steady it. "Of course. My body can die and, when it does, it will be buried here. But, with luck, Philip R. T. Gibbet, Knight of Bithynia—he will live right on. In some other form, in some other time, someday, some other Philip will arrive at the House of the Two Modes, and find the right room— it's on the first floor, in the northwest corner, where the sun shines on the sundial in the afternoon, and the tables are strewn with dazzling knots. But as for me, my body will lie down here, interred and peaceful, until the last story has been told.

"When I saw what Rex had written, at first I thought he wanted me to bring his body here. That is, of course he did—any wraith would have wanted that. *I* would want it. But something made me pause, and I sat there for hours thinking it over. Rex would have known we'd try to bring his body here, anyway. To write that word on the ground at that particular moment—it was for something else. Why did he suddenly need to mention this place at the moment of his death? What had he learned? From whom?"

"Kat," said Kay. "She was the last wraith he saw."

"Exactly. Kat must have told him something. And then she drove a knife into him."

Flip continued on, and they were walking again—slowly. Kay held the lantern as high as she could while Flip studied the floor of the passage. Minute after minute, they carried their little light through the darkness. To Kay, every footfall seemed like the last, every bit of tunnel face, every stretch of rough pebbled floor the same. To left and right, at intervals, they passed the stone-block alcoves; at each of these Flip paused to touch his fingers to the mortar, shook his head, then moved silently on.

"It's no good," he said finally, and stopped. "I've been through this tunnel ten times, and I've not seen a single trace anywhere."

When he looked at her, Kay held his gaze. In his eyes, in the deep points of his pupils, she saw his focus and intensity; in the bruised and slightly sunken skin below his eyes she read the sleeplessness of the last few days, his lonely journey from Pylos, the desperation of his search.

For what?

"Flip," said Kay. She said his name slowly. "What are you looking for?"

He held out his hand, flat as a leaf, palm toward the ground. On the back, between the knuckles, there rested a single jack. Its metal arms caught the yellow light from the lantern, and glistened.

Kay made a sound. It came out of her throat. It was in her mouth. Her tongue made it and her lips shaped it. But it was not a human sound. Her whole body retched. After several seconds she sucked in air, fast, and started speaking words, fast, before she knew what they were.

"That's Ell's jack. She gave it to Rex. In the Pitt. The building—Dad's work. That night. Christmas Eve—"

"It must have been in Rex's hand when he died," Flip said. His voice was as gentle as his hand was still. "Kay, I thought you were down here looking for her, too. But you're not, are you? Why are you down here in the catacombs, Kay?"

"Oidos locked me in."

In a single motion, Flip tossed the jack into the air behind Kay's head, clutched her shoulder with his right hand, snatched the jack with his left, sank to his knees and folded her into an embrace as sure as anything she had ever felt in her life.

"You poor child. I'm sorry," he said. "I'm so sorry. I had no idea. I never thought that—I never thought."

With sudden decision he pushed Kay away. His eyes were lanterns in the lantern light.

"This is very important," he said. "What did Oidos say when she brought you down here? Did she say anything at all?"

Kay tried to remember the staircase—how excited she had been, sure that she would find out who she was and what she was meant to do.

"She said I had to go first, because her legs weren't what they were."

"Nothing else? Kay, think."

Nothing except—

"She said she had a place where, very occasionally, she brought things she wanted to forget. And she said she would have to forget me. And she shut the door."

Just saying it made the tears start again.

The darkness. The terror.

Flip took no notice. "I've been so stupid," he said. "I've been looking down here, in completely the wrong place. I assumed all along that it was Razzio, that it was Ghast, that they *wanted* Ell dispersed. Come on, Kay—run!"

Down passage after passage, back the way they had come, Flip led her, doubled over and loping as fast as his strides could take him in the cramped and narrow space. The lantern flickered and swung wildly behind as Kay raced after him, throwing exaggerated shapes along the rough walls as they passed. At the rockfall that led into the white tunnel, Flip stopped and leaned for a moment to catch his breath. He set the lantern on the passage floor.

"It was Oidos all along. Don't judge her, Kay—don't judge her for this. The bond between them was so strong. She can't face a future without Rex in it. She can't bring herself to look under that shroud, as I did. As Rex so often did."

"What do you mean?" Kay's sides were splitting with the strain of the sprint. But as she gulped air, her head cleared and she knew exactly which shroud Flip had in mind. *The shrouded figure standing in the corner. The future that Oidos will not see.* "Why? What's under the shroud?" *She said Rex had never looked beneath it.*

"You mean you didn't look? The third form of the Primary Fury. Eloise Worth-More, the Wraith of Jacks. I didn't recognize her, Kay—not in the carving, not as she *will be.*" Flip picked up the lantern and began to climb through the opening. "But it's a good thing Rex did. Watch your footing."

He didn't wait for her. He took the passage with long, urgent strides, the lantern held at arm's length before him. His eyes scrutinized every inch of the ground, and when he drew up alongside the last of the alcoves, hard by the end of the passage with its white stone altar, he whistled between his teeth. As Kay drew up beside him, he was tracing his finger along the carved white stone above the vaulted shape of the stone wall.

"She's added this. Oidos. Look."

Where his fingers touched the surface Kay saw three asterisks that had been rudely hammered into the stone by an unsteady hand.

Jacks.

"When Oidos shut you in down here, did she give you a lantern?"

Kay nodded.

"She wanted you to find your sister. She wasn't trying to hurt her, Kay—she was trying to protect her. From Ghast. And I don't think Kat killed Rex that day on Naxos, either. Whatever that means. I think Rex sacrificed himself."

But I saw them fighting, saw them lunging and grappling, as they passed down the narrow causeway. Kay started, a realization breaking on her like a wave. *As they fought, Rex was always on the shore side. He was pushing Kat out to the island. She wasn't attacking him. He was attacking her.*

"But why would he do that?"

"Because your sister has a part to play in whatever is coming, and he knew it. He knew his age was over. He knew it was his time. He knew the hour had arrived for Ell's story." Now Flip was running his fingers along the wet mortar, looking for a place where the gap was wide enough.

"My fingers are too big," he said. "You'll have to do it."

As fast as she could, Kay thrust the tips of her fingers into the narrow gaps between the stones, picking and sliding and dredging out the wet mortar in thick slabs. It fell to the floor as she worked her fingers in and out along each row. Little by little the stones shifted and settled. At length a tiny gap opened at the top. Without waiting to be asked, Flip started working the top stone free, prying and pulling it, straining the tips of his fingers into the space. His face was as hard, as flat as the stone on which he worked. Kay stood back, impatient and desperate.

Flip had shimmied the first stone several centimeters from the wall. Now he dragged it out, allowing it to fall to the floor between his legs.

As he shook the pain from his fingers, still staring at the work to be done, he said, "Oidos was angry with him. With Rex. For leaving her. But she never wanted to hurt your sister. Maybe she needed to hide her from Ghast, but I think she intended for you to find her."

One by one he pulled out the square-cut stones: six, then seven, dragging them out of the wall so that they toppled over one another and away from his legs. Finally the gap was large enough for Kay to peer inside, and with Flip's help she scrambled up and over the wall, to drop into the tight shadows beside her sister, where she lay on a white stone slab.

Her chest was rising and falling in long, peaceful swells.

She was wrapped in a heavy wool blanket. On her stomach lay a slender silver horn.

Kay put her hand to Ell's shoulder, and shook her.

By the time Flip had pulled away the rest of the stones, Kay was sitting next to the stone bed, holding Ell's hand in her lap, caressing it. Tears were streaming down Kay's face, and her skin raced with electricity, with happiness and fear and excitement and relief.

There is too much to feel.

"She doesn't wake up," she said. "Why won't she wake up?"

Flip nodded behind him. Kay looked. Across the passage, in the chiseled white stone, the scene showed a sleeping form—a beautiful woman whose heavy tresses, like branches loaded with fruit and possibility, hung down from the stone bed where she lay. On her stomach lay a horn—the image of that still rising and falling with Ell's breath—and above the scene, in a carved panel, had been cut the words of a short verse. Kay read it aloud by the steady light of the lantern.

THE HORN WILL WAKE THE DREAMER,
AND THE DREAMER WILL WIND THE HORN;
LEAP, HEART, THE WIND WILL CATCH YOU,
AND THE STAR WILL SHOW IN THE MORN.

The words stood proud on the wall in the raking light of the lantern, and Kay read them evenly, as if brushing them like paint on paper with a steady hand. But something about them troubled her, like a persistent bell ringing at a distance.

"The horn of the Primary Fury," said Flip. "The single most sonorous instrument in a world deafened by harmonies. It has gone by many names. The Battle Breaker. The Great Breath of Parnassus. The Pure Noise. The Flower of the Ten Thousand. It has mystical and mathematical properties, of course, but in the end all anyone really needs to understand is the way it sounds—its beauty, its power. It is said that the Bride cannot truly be called, can never be commanded. She goes where she will. But in the voice of the horn of the Primary Fury, we may, as it were, speak to her in her own language." And then, in a gentler tone, as if cupping his words in cotton wool, "It's the partner of the shuttle, whose voice knits up those threads which the horn has scattered to the winds. The one is to the other as sun to moon, as shore to sea, as knowing is to doing."

He picked up the horn with both hands. It caught the light of the lantern where he had set it on the last course of the wall's rough blocks. Even in this tomb of death it shone.

"It belongs to her, now," said Flip, "as it once did to Rex. I think the time has come to wake the dreamer and give her the horn that is hers." He handed it to Kay.

Kay put the horn to her lips and closed her eyes. Taking the deepest breath, her lips pursed tightly against the mouth-piece, she blew a peal that seemed to shake the stone around them. The very air as she blew seemed to condense like dew out of itself, and to run down the face of the world in heavy dark drops. In Kay's ears the rupture burst like a dam breaking, and she felt suddenly that all her life she had been waiting to wake at this call, waiting for a summons to break into her with just such an imperious, irresistible, deafening noise. Around her, like stars falling from the sky at night, flakes of dust and stone rained from the ceiling of the tomb, catching the light of the lantern and shining as they spun to the floor.

As her breath gave out and she lowered the horn, Ell sat up, pushing herself up, rising up, her arms up, her face turned up to the ceiling, like a flower thrusting from the grass at dawn. And then she was in Kay's arms, and the two of them in Flip's, and in the center of the tight embrace Ell shivered and cried, and laughed and was held, and the glow of the light held them together as long as their arms could last, and that was a long time.

To Kay's relief, Ell remembered almost nothing of the long ordeal that had begun in the mountain. Lulled into a trance by murmuring left-wraiths, she could recall since then only snatches of scenes, seen as if through a dream, until the moment Oidos brought her to "this little room with a hard bed." There they had shared a cup of hot chocolate, and Oidos had shown her the horn.

"She told me I was the second most important thing to her in all the world. She promised me that you would come for me,

Kay," said Ell. "And she told me that the horn would be mine. Is it?"

Kay wrapped it in the wool blanket and gave the parcel to her sister.

"We need to get out of here," said Flip. He was adjusting the wick on the lantern. "It will be day soon."

Dawn. When Razzio will launch his balloons for the mountain.

Kay's heart lurched.

"Flip, before Oidos—before I came down here, we had a kind of council of war. Will and Phantastes brought me here because they said that Razzio could help me find Ell, that he could help me find my father. But that's not what he wants to do. He said he was going back to the mountain. He's taking Will and Phantastes, and Oidos and Ontos, and all the causes. They're going to launch a hundred balloons from the garden at dawn. Razzio is angry with Ghast, and he wants to fight."

At that last word Flip tangled his fingers in the flame. Swearing a hot oath, he dropped the lantern and it went out. The darkness fell on them instantly, totally.

"Kay," said Ell. "I'm scared."

"Don't be," she answered, squeezing her sister's hand again. "Flip, what's wrong?"

"We can't let him launch the balloons. It's a trap. This entire house is surrounded by wispers. It took me the better part of a day to find a way through the cordon and slip into the catacombs—and even then I only got through by a fluke. I didn't understand why they were dug in, but now it's only too obvious: Ghast knows what Razzio means to do, and he intends to stop him. But we can't get out the way I got in—all four exits from the catacombs will be heavily guarded." Flip was fiddling with the lamp as he spoke, but it was no use—he set it down slowly, with a quiet emphasis that all three of them understood.

"I see a way out," said Ell. "Follow the star."

She was probably pointing, but in the darkness it took Kay a moment to see what she meant. On the wall opposite, out in the passage, a faint patch of light had appeared. It was no bigger than a handsbreadth, and it seemed to be in the shape of a five-pointed star. Flip, in the passage, saw it right away, and immediately got to his feet. He began to walk down toward the near end of the tunnel. The girls, scrambling cautiously over the low wall, weren't far behind.

"This hole wasn't here twenty minutes ago," he said. He was running his fingers over the edges of a well-defined star-shaped opening in the thin rock wall above the altar.

"Maybe it was the sound of the horn?" Kay asked. "It was so loud—it shook powder off the ceiling down the tunnel—I saw it."

"*The star will show in the morn*," Flip recited. "Maybe."

Kay had frozen. It was there, in the air—she could feel it—*the star—the morn—*

Dad. "*Tell your mother we'll always have Paris.*"

But Flip had another idea. Now he swung a leg up onto the stone altar, crouched, and put two or three fingers through the hole, feeling for something. "There's a door like this in the mountain—it's thousands of years old, and you open it like this—"

Then, whatever had required doing, he did it. Part of the wall behind the altar swung open on a huge pair of iron hinges. Wind rushed through the gap into a little room, where in low light a set of circular steps rose into the ceiling. Flip turned back and held out his hands.

"Leap, hearts," he said, smiling.

They climbed. Kay's heart felt as if it would hammer a

path straight out of her ribs. *Paris.* She felt in her pocket for the little red book. *You'll know where to find me.* At the top of the steps they would have hit a trapdoor, had it not already been open. Ontos was peering down into it, his huge eyes, dark with opiate dilation, surveying the darkness through which they had risen. As they emerged from the stairs into the very center of his dais, in the middle of the garden, he touched the horn in Ell's arms and, from the distant recesses of his oceanic eyes, he smiled.

He had heard it, too.

Given what was going on around him, Kay quickly realized, this was altogether remarkable. Every one of the hundred rooms running around the interior wall of the garden had a glass door. Before every one of these glass doors a paved square, floored with brick or cobbles, led into the building. On each of these hundred plots the causes had tethered their own individual giant hot-air balloon. Every one of them was the same: a small square basket, capable of holding two or three passengers, all of wicker; a small ring of metal equipment; and a huge, swelling envelope—each one a rich, dark blue, the color of a sapphire at evening. Around them the causes swarmed, checking the tethers and halyards, loading supplies, making ready to depart—for the sky above was paling, and dawn could not be more than minutes away.

Just then there was a loud cry from one side of the garden. An answering cry rose from the opposite side. Kay searched first for the one and then the other, her eyes rocketing back and forth, even as her arms fixed on her sister and drew her close before her. Dead center behind the main entrance of the House of the Two Modes, one of the balloons began to lift from the ground. The causes aboard—two—were waving as they rose. Opposite them, in the corresponding place at the back, another balloon was also rising.

"We're too late," Kay said.

"Perhaps we were wrong," said Flip. "Maybe everything will be fine."

"How can everything be fine when Razzio and all the wraiths in the Society are returning to the mountain? How can it be fine if the rest of you are going home, leaving us—" Kay broke off. She searched the faces in the garden for any sign of Razzio, of Will, of Phantastes. At last, in one of the corners, she saw all three of them. They were standing together, watching the ascending balloons.

Kay took Ell's hand, and together they ran through the

garden. There was no one to block her way this time. She and Ell dodged the chairs and tables, ran through the complicated plantings of shrubs and small trees, and reached the corner as Razzio was about to turn in through one of the doors.

"Our young friend," he said to Will and Phantastes. "I told you she would return when she was hungry."

Kay made no time for his jibe. "Razzio," she said. Her tone was serious enough to make him pause on the threshold. "Will. Phantastes. Stop. Call the balloons back. It's a trap. Ghast has laid a trap."

"Kay," said Will. "It's not what we want but—"

"*No*," she insisted. She pulled Ell by the hand, yanking her forward. It was all too fast; they hadn't yet registered.

Now. Pay attention to me now.

They stared at Ell, dumbfounded. Kay stared back at them.

"Hi," said Ell. "I'm awake now. This is a really giant garden."

"Ghast knows what you're planning. There are left-wraiths on every side of the house. They're guarding the exits from the catacombs."

"The cata—" Will was stammering breaths. "Kay, where have you been?"

"Call back the balloons!" She was shouting now. Surely they could hear the fury, the desperation in her voice. Razzio stepped forward off the sill and let go of the door handle. Behind him, Oidos appeared, ashen, at the window. From her expression Kay knew that Flip had stepped up behind her.

"You," said Will. "How—"

"She's right," said Flip. "She's telling the truth. I came in through the catacombs, and they're heavily guarded. If someone hadn't knocked out one of the patrols, I'd never have made it myself."

"He saved Ell," said Kay. Will was stepping toward Flip. As was Phantastes. "He saved me."

But there was nothing to fear. The three wraiths fell upon one another in an embrace that testified beyond doubt the affection that they had always had, and would always have, for one another. Their arms were still entangled when the dawn sky burst into flame.

It was the first of the balloons. It had risen four or five hundred meters into the air. Now the two wraiths aboard the basket were waving their arms and screaming. The basket was dropping fast as fire tore through the envelope. The balloon disappeared over the far edge of the building.

Dead.

"Call back the other balloon," said Kay. She hurled her voice at Razzio, level and commanding. "Make them land."

It was too late. A loud shot rang in the silent air over the garden, and the other balloon burst into flame. Two hundred wraiths and more watched as the basket drifted for a moment, suspended in the burning orange air, then plummeted behind the house.

"He *dares!*" shouted Razzio. "He *dares!*"

"We're not going to the mountain," said Will. "Ground the balloons. If we launch them, every cause in the garden will die."

Oidos had come to the door and opened it. "There is no other way to escape," she said. "Will we live as prisoners in our own house?"

"Would you rather die?" Kay shot back. "Which future don't you want for us now?"

"If we can find a way past the guards in the catacombs," said Flip, "I can get us out."

Razzio, Phantastes and Will turned toward Flip, as one. Oidos slammed the door and disappeared into the house. Kay knew that Ontos must have been watching intently from his dais in the center of the garden, because every one of the causes had paused, and turned, and now stared at them.

"It's risky. We'd need a few things from the house to set up a diversion. But we can leave the causes here, for now, and the four of us—"

"The six of us," said Kay.

"The six of us could maybe thread through the guards at the southern exit. The tunnel ends near a stand of ash and pine trees there—there's cover."

"And what would we do once we escaped?" snarled Razzio.

"I know where my father is," said Kay. "Take me to Paris. All of you. Take me there. Flip will get us out, and I will find my father."

Kay stepped into the middle of the little group of stunned wraiths, pulling Ell tightly by the hand. She knew that this was her moment, the moment in which she could seize or lose her chance, once and for all. "This isn't your story, Razzio. It was never your story, and it isn't mine, either. Maybe it doesn't belong to any of us. But I know one thing for certain, and that is, we must never, never, *never* let it be Ghast's story. I know my father is in Paris. I know it's where they left him, as surely as you know yourselves when you go into your rooms in that house."

Kay held up her sister's hand, and Flip smiled. He reached into his pocket, took out the jack and placed it there.

Ell almost laughed—an impish, powerful grin—and then she flicked the jack high into the air so that it spun in a circle, and then caught it with a flourish in her coat pocket. She stood up smartly, the horn still tucked in the crook of her other elbow, as if she were reporting for duty.

"This little girl is the third form of the Primary Fury," said Kay. "I'd say she's wearing it pretty well. My father is the Builder. I'd say he knows a thing or two about Bithynia. Help me find him. We'll call our own Weave. We'll all go to the Shuttle Hall. If Ghast wants a battle, fine, we'll meet him in the field. And we'll beat him."

"We'll never get past the wispers in the woods," said Will.

"Never," agreed Phantastes.

"Yes, we will," said Flip. He had turned toward the garden. His tone was as tired and torn as anything Kay had ever heard in her life.

While she had been speaking, everything across the garden had changed. All ninety-eight blue balloons had slipped their tethers and were rising into the still morning air. Every last one of the causes had boarded a basket and was sailing into the sky.

No.

"Stop! Stop! Stop!" cried Razzio, running toward Ontos. The mode was circling in the place of pure being, his arms extended level from his shoulders, his feet tight together, his head bowed. His palms he had turned up to the sky as he fanned the causes airward.

"He's sending them to their deaths," said Will. "Why would Ontos do that?"

Flip was studying the balloons as they lifted, a ring of blue giants rubbing shoulders as they caught the southerly wind over the house and drifted, always gaining height, into the lightening sky. He looked at the ground before he answered. "They're all giving their lives for us." His voice had lost its color, and was little more than a whisper. "It's a diversion."

"It's a sacrifice." Will and Kay spoke the same words in the same moment.

"And one we must honor," answered Flip. "Follow me. Quickly."

They sprinted to the center of the garden, taking up food and blankets where they could find them on tables and chairs as they went. Every footstep shot through Kay's heart like a knife. Phantastes tackled Razzio along the way, and dragged him to the dais. Within a minute they were all standing on the platform, heaving for breath beside Ontos, shouldering their bags, twitching, nervous—and yet somehow lingering there to watch the slow agony of dawn break like a blue wave over the House of the Two Modes.

"I'm staying another minute," said Will.

"And I." Phantastes.

And I. Kay took their hands.

Flip's chest heaved as if he were about to argue. But he didn't.

"Fine." He took Ell by the shoulders and began to guide her down the stairs. "But I'm taking this one below. Don't be long. The south tunnel. You know the route. Stay low, and for the love of the muses, run."

A few seconds later, the explosions began. This time there was no screaming; even at this distance they could feel the resoluteness, the calm, the steady purpose of nearly two hundred wraiths sailing for the last time off the board. The balloons were still so close to one another that the fire, kindled in several places, seemed to leap from envelope to envelope, and the whole fleet suddenly erupted into a single giant fireball—a huge orange flame of a star blazing across the morning sky.

"By the air, through the air," whispered Will. He squeezed Kay's hand so hard she thought it might break. "Anything could happen now."

Leap, heart. For the love of the muses.

And they ran.

"**I** gave you strict instructions to wake me."

Ghast glared up at the tall wraith who stood before him. He had woken to the hard rattle of wooden shutters clacking against their frames, wresting wildly against their hinges. Fumbling into consciousness, he had groped with his eyelids for the light of morning, trying to force them open against the wrong dark. It should have been dawn. Light ought to have been streaming into the old stone room from a thousand cracks and slits. But there was nothing—only a storm of wind and occasional waves of what sounded like pelting rain that swept against the outside walls. He had slowly recognized the truth: that it was still night, that it was darkest night, a raging, merciless night. He had bellowed, not in agony but in command, and the door to the chamber had at last swung open. This fawning servant had come to his bedside, handing him a little lamp, then waited.

"Will you eat?" the wraith had asked.

A heaviness in his arms, in his head, had perplexed him as he swung his body round to sit on the edge of the bed. He had known then that the lethargy in his limbs, the wrongness of the dark, the meekness of the servant had meaning. He had felt the bedclothes against his skin: wet, matted, sour.

"I gave you strict instructions to wake me."

"We tried to wake you," said the wraith. "You were not yourself."

Ghast dared not frown. He knew then that he was still not himself, and snatches of what had seemed like an awful nightmare stirred from his memory like monsters surging from a deep ocean. He looked down at a hand that was rising where it seemed he had raised it. It was trembling. He placed it on the lamp, which was hot to the touch. He left it there, burning.

"I will have fruit," he said. "Bring it to me, and another light, and a change of clothes."

The wraith left the room, and Ghast waited as his quick steps sounded away down the long hallway outside, merging into the sound of the storm. He took his hand from the lamp, and smelled as he did so the faint stench of burned skin. He held on to the pain in his hand as if it were a rope pulling him from the deep, from the surging memories of his voice; his voice that had cried out, calling for heads, calling for slaughter, calling for the huddled ruck of settling wings and stabbing beaks of vultures.

Whatever they had seen and heard, it was no matter. Had they been in any doubt before, they would fear him now.

After he had eaten a little plate of fruit and changed into fresh clothes, he draped himself in blankets and sat at a wooden desk in the corner. Two lamps created a pool of steady glowing, and he worked between them. The light and the work staved off the heaves of wind rushing through the valley outside. He had letters to write, business to be transacted in his own hand. Copy after patient copy he drafted and signed, occasionally tearing up imperfect sheets where his grip on the pen had faltered and threatened to soil his authority. Three hours of patient writing. Still the night beat at the shutters; still the light of the lamps steadied him.

"You."

The unheralded arrival of another tall form, after so much solitude, in such a mix of mind and wind, had surprised him. This one was not meek. A gray dawn hung around his heels, where dripping water, too, gathered on the stone floor.

"Oidos has given them the child I delivered to her. The author. The dreamer."

"I know who she is," he spat.

"She has given them the horn."

"And?"

"And we have crushed the plotter forever."

"As I instructed you. I expected nothing else."

"I had expected to meet you downriver, in the marshes——"

"And yet you find me here."

There was a silence. Ghast knew that something had remained unspoken. He clawed at it with his thought, but his face remained a stone. He would not be drawn to ask what his servant must freely deliver.

"The imaginer is with them."

So. Not dead. His resolve buckled for a moment, then held. His face never flickered.

"That is nothing now. I have letters summoning the Weave."

"I will deliver them——"

"In Paris." Within the hour the barge would be moving downriver again. Many of his company had gone ahead to ready the hall at Bithynia for his landing. "We will go now at a doubled pace," he said. "There is very little time."

As he held the packet out to Firedrake, Ghast allowed his gaze to rest on the carved bed behind him. And yet he thought he caught in the corner of his eye a fleeting turn of the wraith's mouth, a flicker of disgust. The light was steady; his eye had not deceived him. The girl, then, the dreamer, had power.

It was no matter. He had laced the hive, and the bees would swarm to it.

6

SPARAGMOS

s the train carriage around her hummed and jostled, Kay fumbled between sleep and wake. She dreamed, and in her dreams images and arguments slid and flowed into one another, all in a turbulent current. She was ahead of herself, looking back with a profound sense of disorientation upon the traumatic events of the early morning. That very day.

Why would he do that? The black smoke rising at dawn.

Her head lolled across field after field, and she murmured intermittent protests. Picking up speed, she felt the train racing north and west, leaving behind Rome and the House of the Two Modes, leaving behind those lawns charred with sacrifice, climbing out of the broad river valleys and back into the mountains and their clear air. Every time the train jolted, Kay woke, felt her speed and remembered where she was. *I am on track for once.*

Escaping from the catacombs had been easier than they expected—easier than they deserved. While descending the staircase from Ontos's dais, Kay had felt strongly that they were captains going gravely belowdecks on a sinking vessel; but once in the tunnels, their pace had quickened. Through those halls of death and burial they had blown like the charge of a blast, hurtling through the rock with their torches thrown out ahead, the light striding with them through the darkness. At the tunnel's exit, framed by an ancient stone archway, the dark rock passage gave out onto a little hill; not twenty meters away a tall wood began, in the winter almost stripped of its leaves, but still—in among the evergreen thickets with which it was fringed—offering the promise of cover.

Just inside the archway Flip and Ell had stood waiting. As they approached, he had motioned for them to be quiet and move softly.

"Two wispers." Kay recalled how Flip had moved his mouth without making a sound. He had pointed out through the open arch—first left, then almost straight ahead. Peering round the wall, Kay had seen something move in the periphery of her vision, but dead ahead could only see a still form lying in the grass—perhaps just a sack or a coat, for nothing was ever as it seemed in the silvery paling of a very early morning.

Those minutes of waiting had been tense. Most of the wispers had moved off, drawn by the flight of the balloons to the north, leaving only these two behind. They knew they could overpower them, even if they were armed, but everything depended on what happened in the intervening twenty meters: would they call for help? If they did, could they run fast enough—could Ell and Kay run fast enough—to slip into the woods without being pursued? Ell had shivered uncontrollably, her muscles sluggish after days of sleep. From his pack Flip had doled out food while the others watched, waited and worried.

And then something inexplicable had happened. An owl had called in the woods—once, then twice, then again. The wisper concealed in the bracken to their left had risen silently, then melted into the ravine that ran eastward around the House of the Two Modes. The other figure lay prone, motionless.

"Now." Flip had pushed them out. There had been no time to hoist their packs or get their bearings. With their heads low they had raced single file directly toward the silent form on the grass.

"Not dead," Will had called back in a volleyed whisper as the girls drew level with Phantastes. "But whoever struck the blow knew exactly what he was doing."

The dent in the wraith's temple had looked about three inches long. The bruise forming around it was straight.

"Someone wants us to escape." Phantastes had crouched by the body to touch his finger to the wound and to gather the wraith's loose robe more tightly around his body. "I daresay help will come for this one before long."

Without another word they had all passed into the wood, threading the thorn trees and the dense-growing bushes at its edge, then disappearing into the mists that still lay heavy upon it.

It had taken the whole day to make their way through the trees, across hills and past houses, on buses and down endless streets along the flat brown river into the city. Kay had thought for sure that they would attract attention, but the wraiths in their robes and cloaks seemed to blend perfectly into the surroundings, especially when the little group, moving fast but wearily, Eloise slung across Will's broad back, reached the ancient heart of Rome. Church after church they had passed, and in among them shrines and ancient temples, decayed, sometimes in ruins, every site swarming with eager faces not skeptical but delighted to see Phantastes's wizened sagacity, Razzio's harrowed despair, Flip's urgent intensity and Will's—

Whatever you are, everyone who sees you loves you.

Kay shifted in her seat, looking through her own dim reflection in the glass. Boarding the train at dusk, the six of them had found a quiet compartment to themselves, and the seats seemed practically luxurious. After hours of waiting in the station—bleak, lined with shops, thrumming with the passing of footsteps, the sweat and sonorities of countless strangers, the slow and creeping cold that comes of sitting still, waiting—the peace of this enclosed space settled around her exhausted body like a warm bath. To her right, Ell nestled neatly into Will's side, exhausted after a day spent rushing through Rome; opposite her, Phantastes and Razzio and Flip were dozing.

And then it happened.

The train, hurtling out of a tunnel, suddenly broke into a broad-sloped valley, huge in its wheel and almost desolate, therefore pristine. The starlight, faint elsewhere, collected on the high snow that crowned the valley's bowl and its sheer rocks, and from that height poured down illumination on the scene below; like milk in a dish it splashed down on a lone house, a single dark structure steaded firmly in its center. And there, for a handful of seconds as they passed through the valley, in lanternly pools where it spilled across the ground, warm, thick, dense, Kay saw light, yellow light: the lights of rooms filled with laughter and song, with close-murmuring embraces and long savors, rooms of love, kindness, patience, integrity and respect. It was as if she had glimpsed, for only five or six beats of her own heart, the eternal heart of everything beautiful upon the earth.

Hot tears welled in her eyes, and she sprang back from the glass as if she had been bitten.

"What did you see in the dark?"

It was Will's voice. Careful of Ell's comfort, he hardly dared turn his head; but his eyes were kind as Kay had ever seen them.

"A home," she whispered. "Someone's home."

And then it passed. Then we went on.

"Do you miss home?"

"No," Kay said. "Well, yes. But I think I miss a home we don't have. A home we never had."

Will was silent. He looked down at Ell's sleeping face

where it lay against his heavy cloak. In the darkness Kay fancied she could just see the warm flush on Ell's cheeks.

"I wish that we could be *together*. Everything about that house I just saw was together. It was filled with light."

Will still did not speak. Then finally he said, "Kay, I'm sorry we took your father away."

"No." She spoke with decision. "Don't be sorry. He was gone long before you took him. For as long as I can remember, we've all—all of us—been *apart*."

Will let a long, slow breath whistle softly between his lips. "Sometimes people who truly love one another can't bear to come together."

"Why?"

"It's too difficult. Where would you go from there?"

"Where would you need to go?" asked Kay.

"Ask a left-wraith," said Will. It almost seemed that he might laugh.

Even in the darkness, Kay couldn't look at Will and say what she wanted to say. She turned back to the window, and spoke.

"Will, that morning before he left, before you took him, before everything went wrong—my father told me that I would know where to find him."

"And do you?" Will asked.

"No," said Kay. "He didn't say that I *did* know. He said I *would*, in the future. That I would *come* to know. I didn't notice at the time—but it was in that little red book—"

"Yes."

"Why did he say that? How did he know that I would need to find him?"

"Don't you always?"

Kay felt that Will wasn't so much asking questions as leading her forward. But she didn't know where they were going.

"Always what?" She traced patterns on the train window with her hand—patterns that weren't there. Patterns that she wished were there.

"Find him. Aren't you always the one who brings him back?"

"Yes," said Kay. Now she turned and looked Will full in the eye. "Yes, I am."

"How do you feel about that?"

"I'm always the one in the middle," she answered.

"Like me," said Will quietly.

"I don't want to be in the middle anymore."

"Do you know what I always say, Kay? The thing I always

tell myself when I have to take that long walk down the center of the Shuttle Hall by myself and leave my friends among the right-wraiths and my friends among the left-wraiths, when I have to pass by the twelve thrones and go to the stiff loom and the hard chair that sits before it, and touch my bruised and blistered fingers to the shuttle, and start to work the warp apart? When the shouts begin and the debate masses like a wave over my head? When the arguments start to flow, laced with taunts and gibes—sometimes merry, sometimes mortal? I bend over my work, alone, knowing that, for the duration of the festival, until the wraiths disperse again into the world as a single fellowship, until the conclave is adjourned and the wispers take up their packs to disappear on the night air, until that moment I am the only thing that binds them. I am their medium. I am their middle."

"And so long as there is a middle, there is a story," said Kay.

"So long as there is a middle, there is a story," agreed Will.

"Will, I'm tired."

"Do you want to sleep?"

"No, I'm not tired like that. I'm awake. I mean, I'm tired of all this. I want to go home, to a home that doesn't exist."

"I'm tired like that, too, Kay." Will was silent for a little while in the darkness. Beneath them the train rushed reassuringly on.

But to what end? Kay wondered as she rode in the quiet.

Phantastes awoke and switched on the overhead light. He leaned forward into the little brilliance that it created. His face looked haggard in the night. "I doubt what will happen if we find your father, if we make it to Bithynia. It makes me wonder whether we are ready. Ghast has overpowered the right-wraiths. Perhaps we will not find even a handful to stand against him."

The light had woken Razzio, across from Kay.

He added what they all knew: "I would gladly denounce him now, even before the Weave; but maybe it is too late. The left-wraiths, too, have long been in his power, and now he rules them not with love, but with fear."

Kay had been staring at the window. In the light cast by the little bulb above Phantastes's head, the thick pane seemed to double her face, and she stared at the two overlapping versions of herself.

"I can do it." She announced it briskly and confidently, as if they had asked her the question. Perhaps she had asked it of herself. "I can find my father. I can bring him back to himself. We can do the integration. I can do it."

I have no idea what I am saying. But I know I am right. I feel it. Anything can happen now.

Will protested. They all did. Kay didn't listen. She thought of herself smiling at their disbelief; in the window's altered face she could almost see it.

"Kay." It was Flip. He had been watching silently. Now he spoke out of the shadows, almost as if he couldn't bear to join the little lighted circle. "I read the order sheet, the day Ghast enrolled it in the Dispersals Room. The thing is, it wasn't just a dispersal. It was a full sparagmos—irreversible. Like all of us—like you—I've been hoping against hope that we might find some way. I've been afraid to look at the truth: there's no going back."

"I don't understand that word, *sparagmos*," Kay said. "In Alexandria it was all possible. Tell me what has changed."

For what seemed like a very long time Phantastes stared at her in the gloom, his eyes anything but soft and merry, as they had been in the subterranean vaults of the Temple of Osiris in Alexandria. He looked abruptly ancient, as if the events of the day before had taken him to the edge of an awful cliff—and he had fallen off. As he began to answer her, Kay noticed that

Razzio, beside him, was shuffling stones in a closed fist.

"There are different degrees of dispersal, Kay—even a kind of spectrum. In the insignificant cases it is enough for the removal and dispersal merely to shake a person from her or his path. Here we take up the thread of a life and fray it, shake it, twist it, perhaps splice it. We meddle with the course, but do not stop the flow. In other cases the process is more far-reaching, more substantial. Here we take up the story and we break it, or bind it to a new story, or even cut it off. But even this extreme form—where we snap away and tear off the future of a narrative, and finish it completely—is not the absolute end of that person's thread; because, if you know that thread and you know how to weave a story, you can return to it and start it anew. You can eke it out, graft it together, make it whole again. You have something to work with. But in the case of sparagmos, there the thread is not simply cut and the course impeded. There the bed is dug up. There the thread is burned. Nothing is left. There is no stump from which to coax an afterlife or second beginning. Sparagmos is final. Even Asclepius, in the heady days of the great rebirths, could not remake a full unmaking. There were times when even he sat down and despaired."

Liars. Over and over you lie to me. But it doesn't matter.

"But Will said—"

"There is one circumstance in which a full sparagmos is thought to be reversible, and one only. If the Bride herself were to gather up the scattered fragments of a life and breathe into it new motion, it is said that she might make something of nothing, and graft being onto absence. In this way Isis once gathered the parts of Osiris after the god Set had dismembered him and scattered the pieces across the earth. It is said that she remade him. But we simply don't know. It's a story, a belief, a myth, an assumption. But then, who is there who knows the Bride, her ways, her powers? Has anyone sat with her under the spreading plane and learned her mysteries? Has anyone questioned her, as you question me now? Has anyone among us, perished in the endless night of madness, felt the healing power of the Bridestone, or seen the milk-light of its twelve-pointed star? No. You have heard the song, you have sung it—'the star will show in the morn.' But the song is all we have. If we know that she can do this, we know it only because we have not had occasion to disprove it."

Fine. Have it your way. And yet I will do it. Kay felt the conviction surge in her body, like a muscle flexing.

"But how does a dispersal take place? How does a sparagmos take place? I want to know."

The old wraith looked at her sharply. "It is not a thing that a child should see, even in her imagination."

"A lot of the things that have happened lately are things I ought not to have seen. I feel a thing, a thing that I *am*, that I can *do*. I have felt it since I stood in the place of pure being. I am asking you to tell me what it is. I need to know."

Kay looked around from face to face. They all seemed about to say something.

"When a wraith knows everything there is to know about a person's life, about her mind or his ambitions, about her fears or his weaknesses, about the things she loves and the things he knows—then the wraith knows how to undo them, how to negate them, how to undermine them. In a dispersal, the wraith seizes on one, or many, or all these elements as if they were filaments in the thread of the life, and pulls. They unravel. The mind comes apart."

"Then my father isn't—You mean he's not *dead*?"

"He's worse than dead, Kay. He has been tortured beyond his ability to withstand it. He's mad."

"And he can't get better. You're saying that he can't get better." Kay's tone was practical, searching. She would press them. Push them.

Make them reach.

"I don't tend to say that things are impossible. But if Foliot and Firedrake performed a full sparagmos, they will have twisted the knife in every corner of his mind, and there will be no part of his being that is not rent and scattered."

"And in an integration, normally—"

"Well, as you saw in Alexandria. You have known all along. A wraith—and it has to be a skilled one like Will—can meditate, and course back through the motives and causes of a life, as if with plotting stones or the threads in a knot, and find the story that will rebind or regraft the thoughts and feelings, the assumptions and first principles that have been broken. Will thought he knew then what they had done to your father, and he was looking for that one clue that would show him which story to tell. Because if we had found your father, then Will might have told him the story that would bring him out of his madness, the way an antidote dispels a poison or soap clears away grime. But Ghast outplotted us.

"We just don't know how to approach a sparagmos. We

were clutching at straws. We are clutching at them now. It's such a serious thing, Kay—almost a sacred thing. It is the destruction not of a life, but of a world. The broken sparagmotic does not keep the madness within, but spreads it, pouring it out into any and all receptive minds. He reels through the world not only broken but breaking. It is almost uncontrollable, a desperate and a dire thing; something that Ghast would never have dared to do in the old days, in Bithynia. That he has done it now means he believes himself untouchable. And it suggests that he really does want to destroy the world around us—at least, he wants to change it permanently."

"But the Bride—"

"The Bride, child—what we mean when we talk about summoning the Bride—it's about a feeling, about sharing a feeling, about every wraith in the hall having the same sense of a luminous and overbinding presence, the sense of an enablement. It's about everyone *believing*, all at once. They believe that they are wedded to the world! But you can't *make* people believe. They have to come to it themselves. These things you want, Kay—they are colossal improbabilities. We don't know *how* to do what we want to do."

"But say we could, just say we could. If we knew where

Foliot and Firedrake left my father, surely we could find him through plotting? And then Will could talk to him and tell him stories like that old poet in the myths, and—"

Phantastes shook his head slowly, pressing his long fingers against his knees. His face passed in and out of the light, like a huge pendulum beating out an eternal refusal. "No, child. Plotting works by reason, and the necessary movement from cause to effect. It follows patterns. Even I know that. But the sparagmotic is no more reasonable than chaos itself. He is borne on a current of madness, as if he were headless, and he chants a melody that is beyond form. Plotting cannot reach after him."

And besides, said Razzio's haggard eyes, *all the causes in the world fell burning from the sky, and are gone.*

For all that, for all his eyes, Kay still felt with every fiber of her being that she was right. Against reason, she felt it. Against experience, she felt it. Against the world and all that was in it, like a miracle, she felt it.

"Then we will do the reverse of plotting. We'll take every step the wrong way. Can't you *imagine* a way out of this?"

"Of course I can imagine. But I wouldn't know what I was imagining. The madness of sparagmos is not the reverse of the pattern; it is *everything but* the pattern—an infinite range of non-being, in every direction, for everything that is. It's not just a shadow but a comprehensive darkness. You can no more predict it than you can explain the cause of all causes. Sparagmos, without the Bride, is final."

"Kay doesn't think asparagus moss is final. And that's final." No one had noticed that Ell had woken, that she had been watching the conversation with the fascination of a kitten, new eyed.

In the double face of the window, Kay almost thought she saw herself laughing, and because she thought so, she just about did. The train answered her with a long, stomach-churning curve. She sat up.

That thing Phantastes said—the night isn't all bad. You can look on the night and see expectation, promise, as great a significance as you could ever hope for. At night, looking can be longing. The star will show in the morn—and stars are there.

It took Kay only a few minutes to convince them. She told them what had happened on the dais, in the place of pure being, when she had seen and felt the power of the cause of all causes. How, for a moment, she had been not in one but two places, seen not one but two worlds, how she had been at once both far and near, both subject and object of her own regarding. She told them how she had been and not been at the same time, how she had suffered sparagmos. How she had integrated herself anew.

I will perform a sparagmos on myself. I will go again into the place of pure being, to the place where everything dissolves and is one, and then I will return. I will know what my father knows. I will know where he is. I will find him there, and I will bring him back to himself. And then I will bring him home.

The landing was built of stone quarried in the mountain. The barge came to rest snugly against it, and was still. After the rough passage through the storm, its stillness was to be savored. Ghast sat, then, at rest in his throne. Soon he would have the title that the throne implied. Then he would destroy this landing, with the quaintly intricate carvings that ran unchecked around its storied walls. From every face of the eastern gate the form of the First Wraith danced. This was unquestionably his place, his temple, the seat of his lost power. If it had been possible to move Ghast to any emotion, he might have felt rage. Instead he felt the foretaste of his final victory. It tasted of steel.

The exhausted wraiths drew their long poles out of the water and, while they still dripped with the river, ran them one to each side through the slots cut into the throne. Two to each end of each pole, they lifted him and bore him on to the landing; river water dripped from the throne as they passed. The light was falling now, and in the shadows antic shapes gathered and recoiled in the carved walls of the eastern gate. Ghast forced himself to watch them as they passed. His servants were now bearing him along the ancient ramp of the Ring, circling the walls as they ascended toward the height. Twice, then three times they passed through the dark interior of the east tower as they turned, and he felt the chill of the dark stone settle on his skin. Shapes, chill, darkness were nothing to him. Let his arms bristle. He was coming as a conqueror, and would soon have his crown; all this—shapes, chill, darkness—would be his kingdom, to wield as he willed.

From the height of the walls, in the last of the evening's red light, he finally looked down on the Shuttle Hall, the library, the Bindery, the Imaginary and the vast dormitories. Beyond lay the overgrown mulberry orchards, long left untended and draped thick with ungathered silk. He felt no affection for these crumbling shells of an antiquated order. Soon he would have them all destroyed. He would erect in their place the more functional offices his clerks had designed. He would require many fewer wraiths than in the past. And their duties would be somewhat lighter. They would operate the machines that made the stories.

He had sent his letters. He thought of them coursing through the air, landing in the hands of their recipients, drawing them back to Bithynia. He thought of the movement of the Weave, and of the shuttle writhing through the warp of the fabric, back and *forth, almost faster than the eye could pick it out. His was the hand, his the movement in the fabric. He looked at his hands, reddish in the light of the setting sun, and for a moment they looked like worms turning in the soil. It disgusted him. But he would be king of this, too.*

7

LEAVES

Kay looked out the window. She thought they must be about to arrive: a sort of gray cast hung over the buildings they passed, and though there was greenery and some open space, its order and symmetry made it obvious that it was the greenery and open space of a city. Kay jostled Ell awake, and the two girls rubbed their eyes and stretched their feet, pushing out the kinks and aches.

"Ell," Kay said. "I think we're in Paris. We're going to have to get out and walk again for a while."

"Okay, oh Kay," said Ell. *That old, bad joke. Imp.* "Kay," she said, and she held her older sister's arm where it lay across her own chest. "Thank you for saving me. I knew you were going to. And I know you're going to get us all home."

Kay squeezed hard, but the tension wasn't all affection. *If I can.*

The two girls got to their feet and clung somewhere to the cloth between Flip and Phantastes; Razzio and Will had gone on ahead, and were already waiting by the carriage door. The train was slowing, and outside, Kay could make out the same frosty pavements and chill, dry air they had left behind in England the week before.

The shock of the familiar northern winter caught her unprepared, and she thought instantly and unguardedly of their mother, surely now out of her mind with worry over her missing husband and daughters. As the train pulled up to the platform, Kay noticed people waiting to board another train on the next track over. Here and there a family stood close together, clutching satchels and sometimes one another. Kay felt tears standing in her eyes, and looked away at a panel of blinking lights on the rear wall of the carriage. *I know what I have to do,* she told herself. *I only have to find him. I only have to find him, and the rest will follow.*

The air outside the train rushed in at them as soon as the doors opened. It was every bit as cold as it had looked; even bundled within the hairy anoraks Oidos had rustled up from a well-remembered room, they were only small, tired children, and they shivered almost uncontrollably. The station around them, barrel-vaulted by huge steel and glass arcs, crawled with trains and their passengers, and the wraiths took trouble to bring the girls safely and quickly through the crowds, up a grand stone staircase and out through an arcade of shops into the street. Flip led with his loping gait, trailing Phantastes and Razzio some way behind, and Will brought up the rear with the girls. Kay noticed that Flip seemed enormously confident in these streets, as if he had walked them many times before, and so knew exactly where to cut a corner, where to look for an oncoming car, where to slow down or stop in order to keep his followers with him. She observed that many of the buildings they passed stood forbidding and proud—but empty and dark. For all that, though, they had a kind of human sternness, which made Kay shiver a little harder.

After about twenty minutes of breathless walking, the girls crossed a wide but drab square and suddenly found themselves next to a river. "The Seine," Will said as he scooped Ell up for a better look over the embankment. "Watch yourself here—this is where it will get interesting, especially if we're not alone."

Kay kept moving across the bridge, just to keep warm,

and Will and Ell followed. The others were still slightly strung out ahead of them, with Flip well in the lead, already turning a corner and disappearing behind the grand facade of a monumental public building, all of white stone. In sixty steps Kay had reached it, and found herself turning into what looked like an abandoned parking lot. Towering nearby she could see the buttressed tower of a huge church. "Is that where we're going?" she asked, pointing up to it as Will rounded the corner. "Not today," he said. "That's the cathedral. We're just going to the chapel."

The others were nowhere to be seen. Will took the hands of the two girls and led them on past a parked car and through a low, narrowly arched wooden door in a wall that, for its unremarkably flat gray aspect, Kay had hardly even noticed. Beyond a short course of steps and through another low stone doorway the girls spilled into a dim, damp room with a low ceiling. "Not here," said Will simply, and held open another tiny door—so small that Kay hardly thought he would be able to fold himself through it. Ell first, the girls ascended by narrow spiral stairs, the stone heavily worn at the center of each sagging step. Kay counted the treads: seventeen to the top.

The tall chapel onto which the stairs gave way seemed at first to be built entirely of colored light: not only did rich blues and reds cascade over the walls, but the very air seemed impregnated with color, and glowed in the beams of suddenly warm sunshine all around. The ceiling was very high and the chapel long and narrow. Great stained-glass windows, through which the light poured, ran along every side. The two girls turned and turned in the space, soaking up the warmth and the sumptuously velveted air, their arms limp and gesture-less at their sides but their eyes—no longer wind-burned and teary—glazed rather with wonder and admiration. Delicately wrought stone pillars ran up almost like latticework all around the walls and into the vaults of the lofty ceiling; here and there an ornament in the stone or a blemish interrupted the flow, but it didn't matter. The overall effect was of elegance and power, emanating with impossible radiance from the tension between light and stone.

"The Sainte-Chapelle," said Flip, rounding on the girls from the far end of the chapel, where he had been poking his head down another stairwell. "Normally it's packed with tourists, but now it is empty for the Christmas holidays. It's an old royal chapel, built by the Capetian kings—"

"And it's a very handy, quiet place at midwinter for a spar-agmos," finished Will.

Kay stopped turning. "Why here?" she asked.

"You don't want to be disturbed during what you're about to do," Will answered. Razzio and Flip spoke in whispers at a distance. Phantastes was rummaging in his sack. "To work your way back to the first causes of a person's being means untelling a lot of stories, and the process can take many hours, even for the most skilled unravelers. So privacy is important. But if you can get it, a large space like this always amplifies the impact of any imagining."

"No," Kay persisted. "I mean, why *here*? Why in *Paris*? Why did they bring him *here*? If I'm going to do this—I have to know."

Will grimaced. "I haven't thought about much else since yesterday, Kay. Maybe it's random."

"No. It's not. Nothing he does is without purpose. I can feel him, cunning, in my dreams."

Will looked at her as if he were a child caught stealing sweets. "I know. Maybe Ghast is trying to force us away from the mountain, away from Bithynia. I think he's trying to make it impossible for us to summon a Weave."

Kay looked at Will blankly. "Or else he's daring us," she said. *Daring us to believe. Daring us to try. Daring us to leap.*

She let her shoulders slump. *What am I doing?*

"Are you sure you're ready?" he asked.

"Ready," she replied. *I am not ready.*

"You're not ready, are you?" Will put his hands on her shoulders and smiled at her with such vast compassion that Kay was overwhelmed with a desire to hug him. "You don't need to do this," he said, mussing up her hair. "Maybe it's not a good idea."

Kay pushed him away and stood apart. "I'm sure, Will. I know how to lose myself. I've been doing it every day, my whole life. Being ready has exactly nothing to do with it."

Phantastes crossed the chapel with a clutch of dried leaves in his hand. Kay looked at the floor. Between their feet, the stone had been painted with a picture of two wolves staring at a nest which contained three eggs. A goose flew overhead.

"You'll need to choose one of these," said Phantastes softly, all the edge melted from his resonant bass voice. "I'd choose for you, but only the imaginer can know which leaf will be right for her when the time comes."

Kay searched his face. Her eyes were question enough.

"Losing yourself is one thing. But great imaginings have always begun in the sap of the leaves of the great tree of the temple at Byblos. And only the imaginer can choose the leaf that is right for her."

"How am I to know?" Kay asked.

"Look at them and think about what you have to do. Sometimes you won't even know why you know, or what you know. But you'll be drawn to one."

Kay looked at the large, veined, olive-green leaves fanned out in Phantastes's hand. They looked a bit like the bay leaves that grew in a large earthenware pot behind the house at home, but they were larger, more rounded, and even dried were of a much deeper evergreen, and their whitish veins protruded milkily from them—like surf on the sea, she thought. She needed to find her father, to think his thoughts—but not his thoughts at all. She needed to dream his dreams, and to follow the fever of his frenzy. The veins on the leaves stood out in some places more prominently than others, and Kay could almost see in the milk-white veins the foamy saliva of a ranting madman. She traced her fingers over the proffered leaves, grazing the ridges of the veins, and let her touch linger on the nodules where the veins stood out most prominently. Where the spine felt thickest—though not on the largest of the leaves—she pinched and drew the leaf out. She had hardly looked.

"A good choice," Phantastes said kindly, staring at his hands, where Kay saw his veins, too, standing proud against the skin. In her own hand she turned the leaf—and saw that this one was not dried at all, but fresh and supple, covered with tiny hairs, bursting with juice.

"But this leaf—"

"No," Phantastes interrupted her. "This is not one of the old store. This leaf I myself picked from the tree, in Alexandria—only yesterday—for this—" He had no more words. Every nerve in Kay's body hummed.

"Oh, Phantastes," she said, and twirled and twirled the supple fabric of the leaf between her thumb and forefinger, dizzy with it, drunk already on its moment.

"Trace the veins back to the stem, Kay. Follow the milk of the leaf." And then he slipped away.

Will was sitting beside Ell, talking quietly about the colors of the glass above them. Kay saw that he had the horn in his hand, where he held it unobtrusively just outside their conversation. She knew what it was for, and that Ell would have to blow it when the time came; and, thinking that the time had better come sooner than later, she sat down and thrust the leaf all at once into her mouth, squeezing her eyes shut and sinking down cross-legged onto the floor. She only just had time to place her palms on her knees before a bitter rush of metal spiked beneath her tongue and seemed to course like electricity through her nerves. Her toes throbbed.

For a few moments Kay swam, just keeping her head above the level and taking in the metal flavor that began to soak first her joints, then her limbs, then her pelvis and abdomen, rising all the time. She didn't know exactly what she had expected, but somehow thought something would happen to her vision, her head—like when she'd been on the dais. This was, by contrast, a simple taste, and yet one that she could feel not only in her mouth, but all over her body—as if she were bathing in a sea of cold electric soup and her feet were tongues. She was aware that the others were circling her, settling down on the floor around her to watch, and speaking in hushed whispers; but they dwindled from her awareness like candles snuffed by dawn, still burning but shedding no light. Instead this sun of metal rose into her throat, burning and beginning to hum, scattering all the clouds and shadows of thought before it, and leaving only a single light of awareness, a single long and resonant peal of equal sound, condensing all causes and effects into that single, lasting, momentous eternity of presence into which all consequence was instantly absorbed.

But even so, Kay found she could think.

In her thought was the image of her father lying on this floor, staring up into the hued shadows of the stone vault above; she walked toward him with her awareness, each step a shudderingly effortful shedding of distance, and stood over him, peering down at his sunken eyes, the gray stubble of his lank and careworn cheeks, the mottle-pored bone of his nose and the slight movement at the inner edges of his pallid lips as he breathed softly in, then out. How. How to see what he saw, to feel what he felt. Sees. Feels. How. As if she were leaping into the air and diving into a hole in the ground all at once, Kay contorted her mind and let it fall, just heavily enough to alight on his vantage. Her eyes widened; she was staring at the ceiling, exhausted with the effort of approach and thinking nothing at all.

Like a balloon balanced on the point of a pin, Kay felt an unimagined, unarticulated dread of any thought, any movement of perception—all ways might lead to catastrophe. Without allowing this awareness to surface into her consciousness, she felt a muffled command: to settle on just the right thought; the thought that would allow her to follow the thread back not to *where* he had been—she was already there—but to *what* he had been, just on that precipice of the moment before they had turned him out into the street.

She spread herself all over the floor, just knowing its coldness, his coldness, beneath the metallic hum still knifing constantly through her nerves. Despite the cold, she sensed herself too warm, too high, still too gathered, too bound. She remembered what Phantastes had said: she should follow the vein, follow the milk of the leaf. With a subdued but sudden sense of surprise, she realized that the leaf still lay whole between her tongue and palate; all the silver seeping through her nerves was the taste of its skin. With immediate resolve, she chewed it, and felt instantly the pulpy, woody paste of the leaf sap dropping fluidly onto her gums. Its taste was richer, deeper, more of garlic and roots that grow in the ground, and in her mind the current flow opened, as if the metal were running to the wood, and the wood running to the ground. Suddenly there were worms. Fingerfuls of them. Kay felt her body shudder, her mouth recoiling from the leaf. It was too much, it would be too much. As if from a great distance, she could feel her stomach heave. The worms turned, crawling like reaching fingers up from her abdomen, crawling into her thoughts, pushing with eating mouths into her throat. They were rising red into a red sun. A scream built in her mind. Unlike the scream of a voice, it needed no breath to sustain it, and it went on and on. She swallowed, tasting the leaf in her mouth. She swallowed, like a fist pushing down the worms where they climbed. They rose. Again she swallowed, remembering something—something bitter and terrible, as if from a nightmare—but determined not to let the memory reach her.

Here the scream ended. Here where the sap dived into the ground Kay at last felt the cold, like a kind of despair not wrapping but enclosing her sense as it pushed, in fluid beads, between the small stones, the beginning of thoughts—not her thinking, or his thinking, but the possibility of thinking. *Think.* She had been on the surface of the leaf, the leaf like a page, and the page that of a book; then by the margin she had sunk to its stem, gathering in; and now she was burrowing within the opening, down to the threads of the stitching where they looped and tunneled in the unliving earth, through the binding, and then out. Here it begins. Here begins. *Here.*

This is it. I realize. In the moment he was—thinking—nothing but this—

Thinking that he had been set apart, cut off, left alone; but thinking also that he had become joined, too, by this unraveling, this unstemming, this unstorying—joined to a cause—joined to a first matter of earth—joined to them all—joined to all. Thinking he was apart, he was together; he was impossibly far away, right here. On the one hand he was single, alone, himself, cut off and discrete; on the other hand he had become real, timeless, like a wraith, as large and encompassing as an idea, universal.

Kay held the singularity and the universality in the two hands of her thought and traveled upward, back into the stem and trunk of state that joined cause to effect, the accident to its consequence, root to fruit. She knew she had to issue from every vein at once, simultaneously; she had to hold the two currents together, not only through this central shaft, where it was so snug, so compact, so easy to twine them, but out explosively into the branch and leaf and text and texture of every least vein, every least vein that was a moment. With a huge breathing swell, she forced her thought out along every available and imagined taste, sound, sight, touch and scent at once.

Come home.

Just before she felt the sound of the horn goring into her stomach like a tusk, shattering her concentration, she seemed to feel herself coming to herself from a great distance, running inward as a wind cut through her; and she knew the place, the posture, the sense of it. *Muttering; a door dug into an earthen wall; light, but also stench; breeze, but also a heaviness; black pavement below, white stone above; concord.*

With a sigh of exhausted expression, she sank upon the surface of the cold floor, feeling its distinct and angled hardness against her side, her leg, her ankle. The leaf was still in her mouth, and before she opened her eyes she spat it out; a little saliva dribbled sideways down her cheek, and she realized she must be lying with her cheek against the floor. Her stiff hand she tightened. She tested her strength, using the ball of her palm pushing weakly up. There were voices now, and the sound of the horn was a memory, and the voices were pulling her beneath her armpits, each one dragging at her, now here, now there. Or were they hands? She fell into them, and found herself sitting up. She opened her eyes into Ell's.

"Kay, did you hear the horn?" she asked brightly. "Did you hear me blow it? It worked, didn't it? I did it."

Kay smiled and thought to put her hand on Ell's cheek; but it only lifted as far as her sister's arm, so Kay rested it there, almost against Ell's elbow, and squeezed. "You did it."

The wraiths gave her five or ten minutes, some water and

some dried fruit before they began to ask her the questions she was so anxious to answer. Phantastes wanted to know everything she had noticed from the beginning, and although Kay was ready to recount it all, Flip broke in severely and kept the questions short and direct. "She hasn't got the energy and we haven't got the time. If Ghast, or Kat, or any of them know we're here, they'll know why we're here; and if they know why we're here, if they even dream of what we're trying to do, they'll be racing to prevent us from finding him. We've been followed before."

Chastened, Phantastes left the questions to Will and Flip, and instead hovered around Razzio, who, plainly revolted by the whole process, sat hard against the far wall, idly tracing patterns in the worn stone floor. Kay dutifully reconstructed her final impression, trying to recall the minute detail of its clarity, like a white light—bright; so bright she almost could not look at it, even now. It struck her like a dream, something she knew inside and out but had no words to describe, something that could only be experienced, and not detailed; but still she struggled, as if she had been outside rather than within it, and gave them all the details she could.

She mentioned the stench, as of rotting leaves or maybe

sewage; the door framed by rough stone and set into the earthen wall; the two sorts of stone, one perhaps the paving of a road, the other a sculpting stone, almost marble in its smoothness and translucence. She recalled the little breeze, which perhaps she had not felt, but seen stirring in—what?—newspapers? But also a heaviness in the air, as of pressure. A sense of movement she remembered, but also a presence or a stasis. The wraiths could do nothing with it; it didn't lead them anywhere specific. Flip became more and more impatient, his hands stretched taut as he sketched fruitlessly in the air. By contrast Will waited quietly, although he, too, was evidently frustrated—wondering if *he* ought to have tried the integration again, Kay thought; wondering if he ought to have let so young a child risk so much and fail them so completely.

Kay searched through her memory of that moment of apprehension, and tried as hard as she could to particular-ize a little more of it—but it was like trying to tear at granite with her fingernails. Though she was sitting still, she felt her lungs heave, and she gasped after air; a weakness eddied in the muscles of her arms and shoulders; and her head hurt. All she could say, as she at last gave up her attempt at recollection and analysis, was the one word she had almost forgotten: *concord*.

The two wraiths both looked up at her with sudden interest, then at each other. They had heard something in that of which Kay was entirely ignorant, she knew—she could see the excitement and hope on both haggard faces.

"Was that a word you saw or heard during the sparagmos, Kay?" Will asked quietly but urgently.

"No—it was more the word that was hovering over all the things I saw and heard and felt and smelled and tasted—as if they all had a theme or a color to them, and that was it. Concord. It was the last thing I thought before I realized I was hearing the horn."

Flip had already got to his feet, and with a fluid motion slung Ell by both arms up and onto his back; she looked surprised, but clung on with manifest delight. "Let's go," he said—loudly enough that Phantastes and Razzio, ten meters away, heard him and immediately gathered themselves ready to follow. Flip was stooping out through the door and down the near stairs. Kay looked imploringly at Will.

"The Place de la Concorde. It's in the center of the city, not far. It may make sense of some of the things you said—it's worth a try, at least. Anything is worth a try."

"There was something else," said Kay.

Will hesitated. Flip was already gone.

"There were worms. In the leaf. Something I remembered—"

Will placed his hand, his broad hand, like a blanket on her shoulder, as if to say she should not worry. Its warmth radiated down her side like the heat of a fire or the stroke of a healing knife.

Down from the chapel, banging out through the heavy wooden doors, through the court and on to the street, Kay trailed after Razzio with Will beside her. Her legs hung from her waist like withered branches, and something vacant had opened up in her stomach during the dispersal—if that's what it was—in the chapel. She counted out the paces again, forcing herself to throw her legs forward onto the pavement, stride after stride. Will must have noticed her struggling, and when he offered her his back, she took it. After that she was able to give more attention to the streets and buildings they were passing: first, row after row of massive white stone piles, even during these quiet holidays guarded by soldiers and non-uniformed sentries; then the river again, which they crossed by an old bridge with an ornamented stone balustrade running down both sides. A few low boats—almost like canal boats—were moving lazily up and down the river, and though it was cold and the doors were shut tight, Kay could hear the faint sound of music and something like a megaphone.

Beyond that, on the far bank, they passed the front of a giant palace, and the girls, gawking, yearned to dawdle; but the others were far ahead, and Will had to break almost into a canter in order to keep them in sight as they passed through gilt iron gates and into the palace gardens. Pebbles and cold sand crunched underfoot, and the trees stood stark against the crisp, bright sky. A few snow patches lingered in places on the gray-green grass, and clumps of people—tourists and some couples—ambled around the lesser paths and near the huge Ferris wheel that suddenly dominated the garden. Ahead Kay could see a stone obelisk nearing, directly beyond the end of the garden, and something about the color of the stone, as they neared it, made her sure that this must be where they were headed. It was like recognizing an old familiar taste, or smell, delicate but pervasive. Without surprise she noticed that the garden ended in a long flight of steps, and that, to either side, it must meet the street beyond in a sheer wall. Without surprise she observed a thin but constant stream of traffic circulating around the obelisk, which stood serene and stable in its center. Without surprise, as they went down the steps, she felt a sudden cool, dank heaviness surround her, as if they had descended into the earthy shadow of the long swards of turf they had just crossed. *It would be here*, she thought. *It must be here*. She slipped off Will's back, touching down.

And then, as they rounded the corner beyond the gate at the bottom of the steps, there he was. If Kay hadn't been looking for him, she would have walked by without knowing him. Though it was the middle of winter, his face glared red in the morning sunlight as if burned; his hair, normally combed back, stood up here and there in ragged brown tufts; his clothes, rumpled and dirty, only seemed familiar on closer consideration; but, above all, his expressions and gestures were completely alien, as if he were playing out some sort of exaggerated character inversion. And his face and hands were animated: he sat on a low crate by the wall, surrounded by little piles of windblown debris, speaking to himself in an unhurried but unimpeded monotone, and gesticulating in a kind of parody of plotting. Kay might almost have thought him some kind of crazed and destitute performer, had she not known him for himself. And while she wanted to run to him, to hug him and hold on to him until he became himself again, Kay was frightened of him, too.

Will and Flip stopped by her side. Ell, still clasping Flip's shoulders, craned to look at Ned More. "Did I look like that?" Kay asked. "I mean, was I doing those things . . . when . . . before?"

Will placed his hand gently on her shoulder, but didn't take his eye off Edward More. "No, Kay, of course not. Most of the time you just lay very still. Maybe it wasn't the same."

"Yes, it was," Kay said flatly. "I still felt solid, kind of whole, when Ell blew the horn, but I was glimpsing something else—this place, here—and if I had just loosened for a moment—Will, believe me, it was the same. I just didn't finish it."

Flip cut in. "I don't think we should approach him—at least, not quickly, and not all together. I wonder if we should let him see the girls at all. But if we could get Ell and the horn—"

"The horn will be useless here," Will said. "He isn't dreaming." Flip didn't argue, though Phantastes raised his eyebrows and watched the others intently.

"Then what do you recommend?" asked Flip.

"I think we need to do things the old-fashioned way, and trust our strengths," Will said. "Maybe we can make a miracle happen."

Flip was impatient. "We've been through this so many times. There is no way that she—"

"Will." Phantastes had his bag off his shoulder in a heartbeat, and was rummaging in it as he spoke. Kay knew what he was looking for, and her eyes pooled with tears at the thought of it. "Will, I have something of yours that you must take back into your keeping now. I've been carrying it around long enough."

He withdrew from his sack a little satchel, which Kay had almost forgotten about. Now he carefully loosened its buckles, one by one, then took from it a little wooden box she had first seen in a boat on an underground lake in the caverns beneath Alexandria. In the bright midday January sun it seemed so common and trivial a thing that Kay wondered for a second whether her memory was playing tricks on her. Perhaps this wasn't the same wooden box. Perhaps that incredible thing which she had held to her lips, which she had sounded through the ancient caverns beside the tree of Byblos, was all just a false memory, a dream.

"Old friend, now is not the time for—"

"Take it. Now is exactly the time."

Will took the box. Kay's heart beat huge strokes in her throat. He undid the metal hasp, and with one last quizzical look at the old wraith, cracked the two wooden covers apart. Ell's eyes looked ready to pop with absorption, and even Razzio was staring. But no one could have been so surprised, so focused, so overwrought as immediately, as Will had become—the shuttle in his hand.

"But . . . but . . ." he stammered. "Ghast had it thrown into the sea. It should be lying half cased in silt at the bottom of the ocean. I don't understand."

"Oh, I heard all his boasts: I will break the loom, I will throw this and that into the sea. But before I let you surrender it up, I plugged all the holes with wax," Phantastes replied. His brow was furrowed with mischief. "And I hoped desperately. The night after Ghast's barbarisms I took two boats, and we rowed the coast off Bithynia with a net. It's a heavy thing, but the hollow chamber within it must have given it just enough buoyancy; we recovered it after only seven hours."

Kay could see that Will's hand was a natural but also a practiced fit for the shuttle. He spun it absently between his thumb and palm as he wondered, sucking air, and then looked at Edward More. A colossal sadness was clearing from Will's face, parting like a cloud from his features, and he appeared suddenly boyish—blood under his temples, a tip to his ears, hair slightly sparky and a pucker swelling in one of his cheeks. For the first time in days Kay felt an exhilarating surge of unchecked hope.

"Use it, Will. If ever anyone deserved a miracle, it's you."

Will looked to Flip for his approval.

"Do it. It's our best chance now."

Will held the shuttle to his lips as he skirted along the wall toward Kay's father. At first Kay thought he was about to blow it, but after a few steps it became clear that he was whispering to it as he walked. Perhaps, she thought, he was saying a prayer. Flip gently dropped Ell to the ground, and the two girls, with the wraiths in their wake, cautiously followed Will until they were close enough to eavesdrop on what was said. Kay could hear her father talking now, the angry and percussive notes of his monologue punching through the light drone of traffic passing nearby. She couldn't make out individual words, and perhaps there were none to speak of; but the tone and voice, though altered, were his. He gave no sign, as Will sat down a couple of meters away against the wall, that he was aware he had been joined. The girls paced a little way off before cowering into the safety of the wall, almost out of sight. The others settled beside them. And then they all remained completely still for several minutes.

When at last the shuttle sounded, Kay was looking at the obelisk across the road. The note was so thoroughly embedded in the air itself that at first she assumed her mind was playing a trick on her, and she was simply hearing what she had been admiring, seconds before, as the awesome majesty of the obelisk. But this sound, it soon became clear, was of another character: though a single high note, it throbbed with intense overtones that came and went, came and went like a petulant tide. Will's face behind the shuttle and his fists lay still and impassive, but the note ached with expression. Kay found herself paralyzed by it, as did her father, whose restive rant came to an abrupt end. He stared about him, as if furtively.

Phantastes leaned over to Kay's ear. "Good choice!" he whispered. "I thought he might go for that on a day like today. The note you sounded. Love." They all settled back and drew their coats over their noses as Will began to speak.

8

THE CLUE

When Theseus came to the city of Knossos, he was only a boy of eighteen, but he had been entrusted with a task on which the whole safety of his father's kingdom depended. Athens, with all its country, had for years been a vassal state to the Cretan king, Minos. Now Minos was a great master of wave and wind. From his island palace he had grown in power and influence, until he was judge over many peoples and nations. These nations he bound to his power by heavy taxes—that is, fines which his subjugate princes paid not only in money, but in human lives. To his palace at Knossos annually the richer cities of Greece sent their tribute in oil, fish, pottery and gold. They also sent their children: the foremost among the boys and girls of every city, who entered the gates of Minos's palace in chains, and never departed after. It was said that he let them loose in his legendary labyrinth, a maze of winding tunnels built all of stone, at the center of which was situated the lair of the Minotaur, a gigantic and fabulous beast with the body of a man and the head of a bull. Perhaps this monster existed. Perhaps this monster devoured the children. All that was known was that they never again returned to their homes, to their parents.

King Aegeus ruled over the richest and most powerful city in all of Greece, and the bloody conquest of his Athens was the brightest jewel in Minos's awful crown. The proudest horses are broken only with the cruelest whipping, and so it was with Aegeus: to him and to his city Minos reserved the most terrible of tributes, demanding the yearly surrender of so many goods, so much lustrous metal, so many fired pots and painted vases, that in a short time he beggared the kingdom. All this Athens might have survived. What it could not bear was the annual harvest of its youth: fourteen of the fairest and most promising children of the city, picked out by Minos's lieutenants, shackled in sober rows on his galleys and shipped into the swallowing sea. In five years the city had grown somber and quiet; after ten years it was little more than a wasteland. The citizens went about their daily business like stick figures in an empty dream. Fishermen lost their catches. Musicians forgot their notes. Buildings began to crumble.

Aegeus had no hope, but he had a son, and in the twelfth year of the Cretan tyranny, this son, Theseus, was selected by Minos's agents to be sent across the sea, sacrificed and fed to the Minotaur. Theseus, too, had no hope, but he had beauty, and when the galleys arrived in Knossos and he was delivered into the hands of Minos's palace officers, it happened that the eye of the young princess, Minos's only daughter, Ariadne, fell upon him. Her eye fell upon him as the pale sky falls upon the morning, when frost lies on the land and no birds sing. The touch of her glance alighted here and there, on this eye and the chiseled turn of that high cheek, upon his dark hair and the new brawn of his arm, on the fullness of his lip and the dusty furze of his thigh. But like the dawn, her particular glance sheeted and enveloped him, too; and who can find himself bathed by such a light, and not search for the lamp that made it? She drew him like a thread; and he who was illuminated by her gaze, at last found out the source of that radiance. Their eyes met. Each looked. Each was looked upon. For that moment each was nothing but that look.

In those days no woman in the Greek world was reputed so fair, so royal as the Cretan princess Ariadne. Poets adorned her with their epithets: she of the white arms, she of the flashing eyes, she of the burnished hair, she with fingers fast as flights of arrows, she with skin clear as the cream of goats. Her circling arms were a king's cradle, her voice his well-tuned lyre, her broad and unclouded brow the fair field of his fortunes. Poets sang these songs of her. In truth her beauty dazzled all who looked on her; but for all her outward ornament, the real ground and substance of her glories was inward, in her mind and in her heroic soul. She knew her own true worth; others grasped clutchingly only at an outward shadow.

Chief among those who misprized Ariadne was her father. At first she was to him a jewel, which he was content to wear among the other jewels of his crown, the better to show off his majesty. But as she grew and matured, he doted upon her ever more and more until—when she had become a woman—the services and honor he offered her amounted to nothing less than idolatry. Ariadne was the most precious thing in his life. She was the whole sum of his cares and achievements, the only object of his happiness. Without her he could not stir, not even to dine or to pastimes. At affairs of state he was naked unless she stood by his side. When decisions were made, either she graced the proceedings or they did not proceed. She was his life, his everything.

To be cherished so absolutely may seem a blessing. Sometimes it can be a curse. Ariadne found herself imprisoned in the love of her father, the admiration of his court, the devotion of many nations. Not one man saw her for who she was or—what was worse—for who she might become. In days to come, no other woman, not even Helen of Troy, would live so bound, so shackled, to every man's need, made into the sign and the symbol of their honor and their fortune. Ariadne passed the nights in the darkness of sleep, but she woke into a greater darkness that was all-consuming. Her life was a maze, a tunneling, in which she wandered blindly with no hope of escape. It was said that Minos's queen, Pasiphaë, had borne at Ariadne's birth another child, the Minotaur, a monster sired not by her husband but by the bull of Poseidon. To Ariadne, this beast that laired at the center of the labyrinth, this brother, this terrifying half god that ate up the beauty of her father's imperial sway, was her twin. She felt herself to be imprisoned in the dark tunnels of its mazy monstrousness. All the world thought her happy; in truth, her life was a silent horror.

When Ariadne's look fell upon the beauty of Theseus, she saw in him as in a crushing fall of rock the power of his hopeless ambition. He had an insatiable appetite to prove himself by doing something impossible, to survive the Minotaur and to deliver his people from their bondage. But in him she also saw her own deliverance, a choice that she might make, the chance to be more than an ornament or an icon, the chance to plot. She saw the chance to create her own story.

On the night before he was to be led into the labyrinth and sacrificed to the Minotaur, Ariadne put into Theseus's hands what is known as a clue—a spool of twisted thread, wound tight—and a knife. Theseus knew what to do. Minos's officers came in the morning, before dawn, and roused the young prince not with a kick or a blow to the head, but with a whispered call. The priest poured oil and milk upon his face and loins, and summoned the gods by strange names as he consecrated the victim's flesh and life to their glory. Theseus stood motionless in the paling gloom, saying nothing; for in his mouth he concealed the tightly bound clue, and against the inside of his thigh, beneath his tunic, hung Ariadne's knife. The officers lifted him by the elbows and marched him slowly down the long, straight flight of steps that bowelled below the palace. Before the great bronze door, embossed with the astonishing head of Poseidon's sea-charging bull, they released him, then stepped back to the safety of the dungeon stairs. The priest chanted from the third step. Theseus knelt only a moment on his knee. The door swung with surprising ease when he pushed it. Within, all was darkness; that darkness closed on him like a tomb as he drove the door shut then dropped the long bolt into place. But he walked boldly into the labyrinth, bearing ever toward the center, unspooling the thread behind him. When he reached the monster, there was no struggle. It awaited him like a lover, panting. After they had embraced, he killed it with a soft upward thrust of his blade; and then he followed the thread—back to Ariadne, back to the light and freedom, back to his father's ship, back to Athens. But Ariadne—hers was not a human thread. The gods claimed her.

9

THE BRIDE

At the story's end, Kay discovered herself standing before her father. The cold wind that ran along the wall bit at her fingertips, and she felt dizzy, as if she had been turning cartwheels. She couldn't think how she had come to be standing there—here—when all the time, she thought, she had been sitting with Ell by the wall, listening to Will's story. And she remembered it, down to the last syllable—which in itself was strange because, though it seemed impossible to her even as she thought it, she somehow knew that story herself, and had always known it; it was not as if she knew the words to say, but that she knew the threads that would draw forth from her were the same words that had come from Will. As if she had willed him to speak.

So preoccupied was Kay with her thoughts that she startled to hear her father speak as he turned sharply to Will. "Did you see what I saw?" he demanded, and in his usual voice. Direct, authoritative. Restored.

"I don't know what I saw. I don't believe what I saw," Will immediately replied.

Her father had thrust his face into his palms, and the long tips of his fingers uncurled from his pendent hair, and then, suddenly tensing, dug into his scalp. He sobbed quietly, as Kay had heard her mother sob the week before.

She wanted above all things to throw her arms around him, to bury her face in the warm woolen must of his jacket.

Take us home.

Edward More was a tall, thickset man, but beneath the brawn his muscles, supple and responsive, were sure. And his body, sitting on an old crate, gave nothing to her. In fact, he resisted her approach. His gaze locked into hers across the scant distance that separated them. He eyed her not suspiciously but curiously, as if he were newly appraising her—as if, Kay thought with alarm, she were no longer his daughter.

"It's okay, Dad. Please, let's go home—" she began.

"No, Katharine. Don't you understand what has just

happened? Can't you feel, can't you remember, what you just did?"

Kay looked around. "I must have stood up while Will was telling the story . . . and walked over, that's all," she said hesitantly. She was about to point to Ell and Phantastes and Flip and Razzio, but when she turned to them, even as she began to raise her arm, she saw that something was not right. Ell was cowering in the crook of Flip's arm, and Razzio and Phantastes held her gaze with a kind of stupefaction, but only for a moment; then they turned away. Without looking directly at her, and almost as if feeling self-conscious, Phantastes pushed himself to his feet and crossed silently to where Will and her father sat. He placed his hand very gingerly on Kay's shoulder, as if assuring himself that it was still there, that it was still a shoulder.

What is happening?

"And Ontos let her onto the dais," said Phantastes, almost in a whisper. "We ought to have known then, Will. We ought to have thought."

Kay looked down at herself, her sense of time and place still in disarray. Her battered brown shoes carried the scars of frost and ice, and in a few places nicks and gouges from the hard stone of the mountain. On her instep the alluvial mud of the Nile had caked, leaving streaks that had turned almost white in the cold. There was salt here, too, from the spray of the sea off Patras and, on the lower cuff of her trousers, grass stains she had picked up—where?—in the House of the Two Modes. Tucked in around her waist she could feel the light cotton wad of the robe Will had given her in Alexandria—no, in the air, above Alexandria. She had *flown*. On top of that, this heavy anorak Oidos had dug from an old chest of drawers, a garment perhaps as old as memory, stained with the old wraith's tears. She couldn't take it all in. She felt lean, somehow, and under the tough, stained fabric of her trousers her legs looked more sinewy than she had remembered them. She held out her hands; they seemed the same as ever, though a little cracked and a little scabbed, and red across the knuckles from the cold.

Phantastes, standing just to her left, held out his awkward hands, cupped, as if he would take hers. But he didn't. "Child, do you recall any of what you just said?"

Kay looked up at him, squinting into the wind, for the first time.

"Katharine," said her father, "a moment ago you stood up, walked directly over to me and put your hands on my face. Are you sure you don't remember that?"

"No. I mean, no, I don't remember that."

Why won't anyone touch me?

Her father turned to look at Will, who lifted his head from his hands to reveal a gaze so drawn, eyes so inky, cheeks so lined that Kay's head rushed with an exhilaration that almost made her giggle. "Tell her, Will."

Will held out his hands, palms cupped and facing upward. "Kay, there is something I never told you about the Bride, and the old stories about how she appeared to Orpheus. I think I didn't tell you because I hoped it was true, but I feared that it wasn't." He stopped and closed his hands, looking at them for a long few moments. "It is said that Orpheus spoke of her whispering, spoke of her mouth moving inscrutably as she darted between trees or slid round corners just out of sight. It is said that the whispering touched him in his dreams, and that, where others saw and felt the visions and movements of their dream-thoughts, he heard them, and saw not things but words weaving into and from him. And it is also said that, when he became practiced at inviting the presence of the Bride, and could call her to him almost like a familiar—it is said that he found the words she was whispering to be none other than his own."

Kay stood shivering in the cold breeze. Her father sat very

near her, her sister, too, and she was surrounded by friends she trusted and had come to adore—but instantly she throbbed with a loneliness that coursed through her arms and legs like cold lead pumping from her stomach. She took a step back toward the street and, she remembered, the moving traffic. Though she hardly cared.

"I don't understand. Why are you telling me this?"

"For the past several minutes, Kay, you have been telling the story with me. Using the same words. You weren't repeating what I said—you were just saying the words as I was saying them. All of them. At the same time. You didn't miss one word. And when I tried to stop the story, to change what I was saying, to lose the thread—it was like you knew that, too, and no matter what I did, you were there with me. It seemed almost as if you knew why I was saying what I was saying. More: it seemed as if you were speaking the words through me."

"What does that mean?" Kay's whole exhausted body ached for her father to pick her up and take her home. *Somebody tell me what that means.*

"What I think makes no sense," said Will.

Kay stiffened. "You mean you think that I—"

"No," Will said. "I—"

"Yes," said Phantastes, with decision. "Yes, I do."

"As do I," said Razzio as he got to his feet. "That was a feat I could not have plotted with all the causes in the world."

"Nor a dream I might have imagined with all the leaves of the tree of Byblos."

"It's just . . . Maybe at last we know what you are," said Will.

"I knew you would find me," said Ned More. "Now anything might happen. Now everything is possible."

Kay stared at her father, at his soiled, matted clothing, his filthy hair, his stubbled and exhausted face, his eyes that were once so playful, so generous, so warm. Now they seemed cold, appraising.

This was all on purpose.

From the place where she had been cowering, Ell— uncertain but indomitable—took a few steps toward her father, put out her hand to his coat sleeve and touched it. Kay watched with fascination as he placed his hand firmly on hers, then drew her little sister into a firm hug against the scruff of his shoulder. Her heart yearned to cross the space between them, but it was like a sea, vast and empty. She couldn't go to him.

You set me up. Did you set me up? Rex said I was the one. He knew. You knew. That I am—

She shuddered. *Ariadne. Left in the middle.* Her gaze moved without comprehension across each of the rest of them in turn, from her father and Ell, across Will to Phantastes, to Razzio. She lingered there; the old left-wraith's broad smile was as warm as it was unusual, and Kay knew it, and she wanted to smile back, to take his olive hands, and dance, to cry out for joy, and sing, because this was a triumph, theirs was the victory, hers was the quest's end and it had all been for *something*, they had *done it*—but there was a mass of muscle squeezing the top of her neck, and her whole head felt as if it were a fist tightening.

Ariadne, discarded. The gods claimed her. Hers was not a human thread.

Kay couldn't bear to think, and didn't: in a single movement she turned and walked down the street, away from all of them and back toward the river, following the flow of the cars. Had she wondered whether they would follow her, she wouldn't have cared; but as she walked, her mind was entirely occupied with other sensations, other feelings: the wind, still on the back of her neck; the firmness of the paving stones beneath her thin soles, and the chill of them; the sharp, acid taste of the car exhaust in the rounded curve of her nostrils as she breathed; and under it all, the thin, frail sense of a body that she had thought her own, but which seemed to be something else completely. She wished that the wind would stop blowing her along, and would simply blow through her. She wished it might carry her into the black depths of the silty river.

She took the corners haphazardly, choosing a way and then, as randomly as she could, striking off in the opposite direction whenever the inkling struck her. She was determined not to be determined, and if they would follow her, then at least she would give them a time of it. She longed to sit on a stoop and cry. Yet she always carried on to just one further corner, or across one further intersection, one further trunk-lined park. To stop would be to admit limit; and so, even though she was growing footsore, even though she often longed to sit, or even to lean up against a wall in the reprieve of some shadow, she pressed on, out—past the constraint that, until today, she would have called herself. *Myself.*

On a broad and empty avenue, largely deserted but for the occasional taxi with its droning rush hurtling past her, Kay's legs finally gave out and she crumpled at a bus stop. For three or four minutes she enjoyed the stillness and the sense of relief in her fatigued muscles, and listened to her heart play its rhythm across the motion of her breathing as it slowed.

They would not be coming for her. She was alone. And because she had deliberately avoided pattern, avoided paying attention to her choices, avoided even looking around as she walked, she couldn't remember or gather any sense of her path, no guess at a trail that might lead her back to the place from which she had come. She had felt an overwhelming need to escape from the stories Will had been telling, and to evade and avoid all the elements of those stories, and how they might erase her, shadow her, reduce her. But now she realized: by doing that she had lost her father again. She had lost Ell again. Kay began to cry because no one was there to watch her do it.

Hot sobs boiled out of her, and the tears ran down her face. To be alone. To have run. To have lost them all. She wiped at her tears. This was not what she wanted. Still she cried. As she held the wet cuff of her robe to her face, feeling its cold pressing on her cheek, she seemed to see something very far away—a dark room, a bewildered awakening, a body wrapped in damp blankets, a lamp at the door—and, with a start like the flood of the leaf on her tongue, she remembered her dreams, night after night of them: dreams of her father and of Ghast; dreams of a journey down the river, of Firedrake, of anger, of pride; dreams of a wicked, cold intensity. Dreams of a red light setting on Bithynia.

What does it mean? What can it all mean?

And then, suddenly, as if still in a dream, an incredible thing happened. Down the empty street a bus loomed and rumbled, and the driver, seeing Kay huddled in the glass shelter, began to apply the squealing brakes. Kay turned from the bus as it stopped and the door swung wide: she had no money, no idea where to go, and above all no French. Facing toward the back of the bus, she tried to give the driver the impression that she was not intending to travel. In the back of the bus two or three people sat in different places—in the far rear, under the lights, an old woman with a white bun and dark red lipstick; on the far side, facing her, a dark-skinned boy in a pressed shirt with starched lapels, clutching a rucksack on his lap; and near her, very near her, facing away, a dark shock of long black hair that must belong to a young woman. Kay was looking at her as the driver muttered something, the door swung shut, and the bus's engine began to lumber up into motion again. And that's when the woman turned her face, and through the windows met her gaze.

It was Kat.

The instant she saw her, Kat leaped from her seat, but the bus was already picking up speed, and all she could do was race to the back, fumbling for the bell as she clambered into the rear windows, trying to bring the bus to a halt while, Kay realized, not losing sight of her sudden quarry. Kay's legs recoiled on their exhaustion like springs, and she shot out of the shelter in a panic. At first she simply wanted to get out of sight and to evade that gaze; but as soon as she had thrown herself safely behind the pier of a large office building, she realized she needed to know where and when the bus would make its next stop. As she peered out from behind the stone and watched it slowing, she thought she would turn to run the opposite way, but then it struck her—Kat was a left-wraith, and if she were in Paris, she would be here for one reason only: *she would be on her way to the others.* A stifling gob rose in Kay's throat as she apprehended the danger the others were in, and the complexity of what she would have to do to find them, to save them. The bus had slowed to a stop nearly half a mile down the straight, broad boulevard. Sure enough, only one dark-haired passenger issued onto the pavement and, sure enough, she headed directly back toward Kay, half running and half flying in her haste. *So it will be a game of cat and mouse,* Kay thought. *Hunter-seeker.*

On still weekend days in November, when the fog had settled overnight and hugged the stubbled fields like a damp blanket, Kay and Ell had played along the edge of the trees, darting in and out of visibility in a game that was not quite hide-and-seek. Each sought the other; each evaded the other. The rules were simple, but the action quickly became complex: both hunted and both were prey, and, because the game could only end by surprise, both struggled to keep the other within and just out of sight. It was a game of edges. Now Kay played it again, using a logic that had become instinctive. She moved laterally, down the side street just behind her, but making sure first to weave slightly into the boulevard so that Kat would see her turning. It was crucial that Kat should commit to the long stretch of boulevard between the two of them, and not turn before her—Kay wanted Kat to follow her, and not to intercept her—so she took her time, moving slowly, trying to give the impression that she didn't know that Kat had left the bus, didn't know that Kat was following her. She pretended to be careless, and hoped. Once round the corner and out of sight, she sprinted down the street and then turned left again, doubling back in the direction of the bus, but one block over. So much mist, Kay thought with a little satisfaction, into which she might disappear, and from which she might luringly dart.

The next stage was the slip. This was Kay's favorite part

of the game, and the one at which she was most accomplished. In the field behind the Laundry Farm, where she and her sister had most often played the previous autumn, Kay had so fully perfected the slip that she had almost hesitated to use it, knowing how desperately frustrated it made Ell feel. But her tools there were trees, fogs, hedges and the odd ditch, fence or stile. Here, in contrast, she had buildings, crowds and—just at that moment she picked it out in the distance, three blocks ahead, topped by its oval sign and sinuous lettering—a Métro station. Once she saw this, Kay didn't even need to plan. She had pulled Kat back toward the bus route, drawing her—she hoped—in the direction she had been going. Now, if she could just manage to lose her, Kat might well give up—and go back to whatever she had been doing in the first place.

Down the narrowing street, threading through the casual shoppers with their underarm parcels and their steaming breath, Kay resisted the urge to look behind her, trusting that Kat was still pointing to the quarry. She pretended ease, trying to look relaxed, casual, even as her feet moved quickly under her. There was hardly any traffic on the street, so she stole only the most careless-seeming glance behind her as she crossed over, about a block before the station. She thought she glimpsed

Kat—perhaps running now, but certainly much closer—about a hundred meters away. Kay paused for a moment under the purple awning of a pâtisserie, pretending for the briefest delay to covet some cakes; in reality she was ticking off the seconds as her heart raced, one second to every two, then three beats, letting Kat close the gap, letting her relax into this little snare. Then Kay wheeled around, touched a lamppost with her shaking arm and drove forward, down into the Métro stairs.

The rank, warm smell of rot and urine wafted up as she took the stairs two at a time—now out of sight and again racing a little, making up time to work the slip and listening hard for the sound of a train. The whole art would depend on choosing the right platform—of which, she saw as she came off the stairs, there were four: two pairs on two lines. She had no ticket, but the station was mostly deserted at midday just after the new year, and with a little speed she might clear the stiles (just like in the fields at home) without anyone much taking notice. She hardly thought, but a scramble needs none; and at the small price of a knocked knee, she got away. Now she slowed, still listening hard, trying to pull the sounds of the trains out of their tunnels. There was a faint rumble from somewhere, but which of the two sets of stairs produced it she could not yet tell.

Footsteps, however, she did hear—but too plodding, too heavy to be Kat's. And then another set, this one lighter, quicker, not even but syncopated, as if taking the steps in hurls, and then threading around someone else—and Kay held her posture for a second, but only a second—like a bob on a line, just before the fish bites—and then dropped toward the stairs.

The rumble was growing louder, but Kay was still unsure. She would have to guess, and did. As soon as she was out of sight of the stiles, she threw herself at the stairs, trying to get to the bottom and round the corner before Kat gained them, half sliding with her hands down the rails to either side. Kay heard steps behind her. She walked slowly toward the right-hand tunnel, seeming to check the signs as she ducked into the alcove, as casually as she could. Instantly, behind the shadow of the wall, she sprang again into full flight. She had about seven seconds on her pursuer, and would need to use every one of them if she were to escape this dead end. The platform itself was almost empty, but the rumbling, strangely, seemed a little louder. Kay scanned the tunnel in both directions, looking for lights, for some kind of departure screen, for expectant passengers.

And then she saw it, just beyond a couple holding hands

down by the furthest end of the platform: a dark corridor leading on to a small staircase, marked with the colors of the second line. Below. That was where the sound was coming from. She bolted for the passage. As she gained another stairway, she heard the clack of Kat's heeled shoes behind her. Three by three she dropped down these new stairs, shot over the connecting corridor and round a corner, and then down the last flight. The train was just pulling in below her, and there might just be time to pull it off.

From the connecting corridor Kat would have a full view of the platform for a few seconds before, turning the corner and heading down the stairs, she lost sight of it and Kay disappeared. Kat would see her running and would assume that she had boarded the train. But she wouldn't board the train; a lit blue sign at the end of the platform marked an exit, and if Kay could time it just so, she would slip into the passage just before Kat reached the platform.

If, if, if.

As she flew off the stairs, Kat's heels already ringing on the access bridge that ran above the platform, Kay crossed her fingers. She bounded down beside the train, praying that her white coat was catching the light, that Kat would see her. In her head she counted Kat's paces, accelerating to a sprint. As the footsteps behind her suddenly grew muffled, she leaped into the side passage. Behind her the doors closed and the train began to pull away. Kay stole a glance backward as she heaved pantingly up the stairs and—*Brilliant!* she thought—saw the train pulling forward, away from the sound of Kat's footsteps, now almost drowned by the roar. Kat wouldn't be able to see the empty carriage as it disappeared into the tunnel, nor—she thought as she yanked herself round another corner at the top of the stairs—the quiet-stepping girl as she vanished into the maze of passageways, heading waywardly back toward the light.

But the hunt was hardly over, and Kay sobered quickly. She had to gather her breath and find a safe, invisible hiding place from which to mark her own prey. As she came back up, Kat would quickly reveal whether she had fallen for the lure: if she took the main corridors, slowly and directly heading for the street, Kay would know that she was safe; but if Kat took the smaller side passages, listening for footsteps, the slip would have failed.

Kay bounded up the long flight of stairs before her as quietly and quickly as she could, puffing her cheeks strenuously and pushing down on her aching, wobbly thighs with more than a girl's force. *If I am to be the Bride,* Kay thought grimly to herself, *I'll have to get better at disappearing.*

She gained the level. Up here she would have an easier time of it, she thought: columns stood at regular intervals in a few parts of the station lobby, and she need only skulk in a shadow and then play the circling game. The columns were not much thicker than trees, and Kay was a past professional at the childish sport of trunk-shadowing; without crackling leaves underfoot to give her away, it would be even easier than at home. She chose her column and waited for the clack of those telltale heels.

This left her now on the cusp of the last, easiest part of the course: the flip and chase. With a few more thudding heart strokes and a bit of jittery footwork, Kay was sure it had worked—Kat's footsteps died away as she rounded the corner of the station exit, and Kay could hear them slow as she labored— now tired—up the final set of stairs. She waited until the sound had just died away, and then sprinted after her. So the hunted became the hunter.

Once again in the sunlight, Kay tried hard to get her bear- ings. She had come up a different stairway from the one by which she had entered, and for a moment she spun, terrified, thinking that she had emerged on an entirely different street or forgotten which way she was headed. But then a purple awning a minute's walk away began to shake as the proprietor drew it a bit further out against the sun, and Kay remembered she had noted it for a landmark just before she dashed into the Métro. Kat couldn't have gone far, she decided, and if she wasn't on this street, she would have crossed back to the larger boulevard, perhaps to get the bus again. Kay set off warily, keeping her head moving as she walked, prying with her eyes into every alcove, every storefront, every alley as she passed it. Now that she was the hunter, she must not lose her prey. The street had emptied slightly, or perhaps there were fewer shops along this section, but still there was no sign of Kat moving among the few sparse groups of people. Kay began to panic, and raced to the first corner, hoping to find that Kat had simply turned left.

She hadn't: the tree-lined street, with its two lines of parked cars and its neatly manicured front doors, was completely void of people. Kay spun round, but in the other direction, across the larger road, it was the same. She ran back to the intersection, furious with herself for letting the line slacken, and terrified that Kat would pop out behind her and put the chase back on the other foot. She whirled. A few cars raced past on the street, revving their engines menacingly, and an old man, nearly bumping into Kay as she reeled, stopped short in annoyance, then kept walking. *Down*, she thought—she had to get down, put her head down, keep her advantage. She crashed heavily into a corner beside some newspapers that lay stacked just outside a newsagent's, and huddled there with her back against some aluminum screening. She watched the street frantically.

She couldn't have been luckier. A few doors down, the black hair swept out onto the street from a café, and Kat passed within a meter of Kay, taking the corner to the left from which Kay had just returned. She was carrying a piece of cake wrapped in paper, and taking slow, uneven strides as she ate. Kay counted to twenty, then another ten for good measure, and followed her. The cars would give her cover, she knew, and the emptiness of the street would work to her advantage, now that she was giving chase.

From street to street Kay marked her: on to the boulevard, down a quarter of a mile, left along a park, through a pavilion dominated by weird cube sculptures, and through a maze of tiny back streets, partly cobbled. She made the most of the cover she found, but she hardly needed to worry: Kat had given up thinking about Kay, and seemed completely unaware that she was being tracked. When they came out onto the river, and the wraith began to make for a large bridge, Kay's heart sank and soared at once, for just beyond the bridge was the obelisk she had watched earlier in the morning, but the ground between the bridge and the open plaza, where the obelisk stood, was completely open. No place to hide at all. There was no way she could risk following Kat across the water, though she felt sure that her father, Ell and the others could not be far. Instead, she squatted at a corner, half behind a post, and hoped for the best, watching the black duffel coat and glossy hair slowly disappear into the middle distance.

When Kat had almost vanished on to the far side of the plaza, Kay threaded through the traffic of the busy street and struck out for the wall against which they had sat earlier that morning, hoping to hang as much as she could in its shadow. But she couldn't make up the lost ground, and Kat crossed behind some traffic and turned in behind a bus; when the bus pulled away, she had gone. Kay wondered if she had boarded the bus itself, and she was just about to break into a run when a large arm grabbed her from the right, lifted her fully off the ground and practically hoisted her sideways across the pavement and into the opening door of a parked car.

She might have screamed, but something stiff was shoved up against her face. Instead she kicked, and hard, but because she couldn't see, her legs mostly met air, and her knees shook painfully beneath the caps. The car door slammed behind her, and after a severe bout of jostling and stamping, she got her head free enough to see, and to scream.

She stopped yelling almost as soon as she started, because the face staring into hers from the front was that of Phantastes himself. The arm still clasped warmly about her middle was Flip's, and he gave her a gentle squeeze. "You're a lot heavier than your sister, Kay," he said in a low voice, smiling. "Now get your heads down. Now!"

Phantastes faced forward and slumped down in his seat. Judging from the sleeve she could see, Razzio sat behind the wheel, with a hood drawn over his head. Flip could hardly make himself as inconspicuous as either of them, but he slid down anyway, with his legs lying across the floor of the car, and hunkered as low as he was able.

"We thought you were gone," Flip said. "Just after you walked off, we were ambushed from the wall by about ten of Ghast's most loyal acolytes. Somehow they must not have seen you, but they certainly saw us. We thought we might find some left-wraiths skulking about your father, but not in those numbers, and while we were prepared"—he touched his palm to the long knife belted at his side—"well, we weren't *that* prepared. We scattered. Will took your sister and your father. They ran toward the river. The three of us split up, heading back up the stairs and through the garden. They must have been after Will, because only two of them paid us any attention at all, and between the three of us we lost them. Well, we did more than lose them."

Kay raised her eyebrows. Flip clearly wanted to say more.

"One of the advantages of being a clever left-wraith," he said, "is that a carefully plotted tale is not, in some circumstances, altogether different from a well-orchestrated rumble. They ought to remember very little of our trap when they wake up from their concussions—eh, Phantastes?"

"Boom," said Phantastes with a chuckle.

"But Kat—"

"Yes, we saw her. We certainly didn't expect to see you following her, though! How did you find her?"

"I didn't. I just ran into her. Like a dream. At a bus stop. She tried to catch me, but I gave her the slip. Then I followed her back here. I thought she would lead me to you."

"Smart. Kat's been in Paris a lot, and knows it better than any of us. I'd guess she's organizing Ghast's wispers here, maybe everywhere—though not closely enough to recognize the car we borrowed from those two unfortunate goons of hers. Anyway, she'll almost definitely have gone to Ghast's Paris hide, up on the hill near Montmartre. I think she probably just wanted to take a little walk-through here to see if the place had been cleared."

"But why didn't she recognize you, if she was looking for you? If she's a left-wraith, shouldn't she have figured all this out?" Kay wriggled lower in the seat to take the stress off her back.

"Sure—except that there is one thing the left-wraiths *aren't* plotting for, and it's throwing off all their thinking. If I'm right, it will be the reason why Will and your father and Ell got away on the river."

Kay raised her eyebrows but said nothing. *The river.*

"They would never believe that the Bride has returned," said Flip, beaming, and he rubbed her head furiously. "You're going to blow up in their faces like a bomb!"

Razzio coughed from the front seat. "I might remind you, Flip, that you and I are both left-wraiths."

Flip's smile broadened, if that were possible. "Kay, they're going to love it. By the time you're finished with them, Ghast won't have the loyalty of the least tick crawling on that mangy pelt of his. No one will fear Ghast, then. When they find out that the Bride has returned! We'll run him off the mountain. No, we'll seal him in the mountain, and then we'll leave him there. We'll go back to Bithynia."

Bithynia. A red light over Bithynia.

"I suppose we'll have to," said Razzio, sighing a deep sigh—a sigh with which he seemed to resign all his stratagems and ambitions to lead the Honorable Society. Kay thought she felt the last embers of an ancient enmity cool suddenly, and fall to ash.

"*I suppose we'll have to,*" echoed Phantastes, quietly guffawing.

"And how are they going to find out?" asked Kay. She touched her face and, finding it hot, realized that she had blushed. "I mean, how are they going to find out about the Bride?"

"Well, you'll show them, of course. Razzio, drive."

He stood in the hall, where the banners had been hung according to his instructions. The hearth had been laid ready for the fire. On the dais at the west end, the twelve thrones also stood ready, and before them, like a promise, his own chair of state. Before that, set by his servants into its ancient place in the floor, the iron wheel lay ready for the great consult. Eleven times he had turned it; only one night still remained.

It seemed an age since the Honorable Society had last gathered in the Shuttle Hall. So it was.

The Weave! The Feast of the Twelve Nights!

He yawned.

He walked the length of the hall and counted every step. He returned, and did it again. He would not yet sit on the throne, not in this place. The moment would be all.

The other wraiths were sleeping. It was the dead of night. But he would leave nothing to chance, nothing to the improvisation that the imaginers claimed for an art, but which was no more than chance.

There was one throne that would of course remain empty. He looked at it. It was, after all, a plain wooden chair, not broad, the carved arms low, the back gently curved and not high. It was fashioned of a dark wood—mahogany, he supposed—which gleamed in the light of his lamp as he held it close. It had been empty for as long as he could remember—in fact, one of his earliest memories of the Shuttle Hall was of staring at this chair with a mean eye that he came later to realize had been contempt. It was nothing special, granted; but it had been hers, and she had left it all the same. As a young man, he had stood almost where he stood now, staring at that chair while the others cried out in the throes of story, staring at the loose end, the void, the fault, the little wound.

It was only later, when he was more mature and experienced, that he came to understand that the absence was only a symbol. The right-wraiths could have filled the place, had they wanted to do so. They did not. They preferred in their arrogance to let the chair sit empty, a goad to the left-wraiths, a breezy performance of their own careless self-assurance. The Siege Vacant, they had called it. Pompous fools! How it had galled him to see the First Wraith kneel before that empty chair once a year, at every Twelfth Night, and ask for guidance from a deserter! No more. This should be the last Weave.

He turned to the left, walked the twenty-eight paces to the stalls and took his ancient place among the benches of the left-wraiths. He had not sat here for many years. In the gloom of middle night he could see no further than his lamp could show him, but he felt the old presence of the Shuttle Hall around him all the same, complete. He thought of his pride at first joining the Honorable Society, his anger at discovering how little his kind were esteemed within it, the revenge he had sworn when they called him "scrivener."

Of the twelve sources of story he knew all there was to know. Within quest, three branches; within love, alike three; within chronicle, three; and one each for discovery, for gain and for loss. He knew the character of heroes, the trials of lovers, the cunning of politicians and the strategies of generals. He knew the songs of bards and the idle games of shepherds, the laughter of tricksters and the venom of revengers. All forms of poetry he knew, and every kind of prose. Many of the greatest anthologies, the treasure books and mythologies that now stood in the library in the mountain, he had copied. He had seldom blotted a line, and bore the scars of that precision in the dullness of his eye and the thick mass of locked muscle in his neck. What he had done for the Honorable Society. The pain and toil he had given.

Although a left-wraith by name, he had never cared for the affectations of plotters, for their boards and stones, their talk of the thread and their reverence for their little collection of sacred instruments. He had endured the voice of the shuttle, the braying sandblast of the horn, the clack of the loom. Throughout his youth he had rolled his eyes in private at the talk of snakes and swords. He had said the words, though they almost stuck in his throat. He had tolerated Razzio's hocus-pocus with the two modes. But his patience only went so far.

He placed his hands on the bench beneath him and ran them along the cool grain of the old wood. Its furrows and ridges irritated him, as did the slight concavity where his own body had, over the years, hollowed out his place. These ridges and hollows had nothing to do with his clean copies. His copies had always been exact, and now, locked up in the mountain, they would stay exact forever. He had done everything exactly as it had been required of him. They could never fault him for a single mark out of place.

A new age was coming: a new age in which plotting and imagining would no longer be necessary. He would fill the Shuttle Hall with machines. They would make the stories, now, to a design that Razzio had invented, to a specification that Ghast had himself perfected. Every one would be alike. Every one would be a perfect copy of the other. The world would thank him. The world would thank him handsomely, and he would become incalculably rich with their gratitude.

Ghast took up his lamp and made his way to the vestibule by the entrance. Once behind the curtain, he extinguished his light and stood in the empty silence. It was pure, void and true—untroubled by the ache of hearts, the pounding of fists, the cry of antagonists. It lay as quiet as a grave, ready for the blood that he would spill in it.

10

THE LOOM

The hall fell as silent as the huge oak beams that spanned it, and to the rhythm of their spanning Kay timed her breathing. She fought back a smile that lingered, aching, just behind her eyes, and counted the wooden stalls lined along the two walls to either side of her, and before them the long benches ranked five deep to the aisle the whole length of the hall—to the right the right-wraiths and to the left the left-wraiths. From one end to the other, Kay guessed, seven hundred or more wraiths sat gathered, murmuring expectantly—agitated, even. But why shouldn't they be? The first Twelfth Night, the first Weave, in hundreds of years? Kay threw back her head and, as the hair tressed and bowed over her shoulders, let the smile pour into the tiny diamond lights that studded the ceiling. *To think we have come to Bithynia at last.*

Two days before it hadn't seemed possible. Kay looked vacantly toward the far end where the dais stood with its twelve high thrones, and remembered the tumult of their arrival in Montmartre—how she and Flip and Razzio and Phantastes had tumbled out of the car in a tiny lane on the steep hillside over the city, and she had followed Flip through the low door into a pretty cobbled courtyard, where they heard, faintly, urgent voices—her father's voice among them—passing an argument back and forth like a ticking charge. Up an external stair and into the warm wooden interior she had swept exhaustedly with a kind of bleak hope, dazzled by the thought that she was about to fall into the arms of the wraith who, hours before, had hunted her almost to an end. Her enemy. Their enemy. She had suddenly thought how difficult Flip and Will and Phantastes would find this—to confront, to make truce with, the wraith who had killed Rex.

But perhaps the thrill of the plot had been carrying them, for when they pushed into the low-ceilinged, comfortable room, they had found Will and Ned More seated before the hearth fire, drinking hot cider and arguing animatedly, if urgently, but also respectfully, with Kat.

All that gorgeous black hair. Those gripping eyes.

Murderer, Kay had thought. It hadn't mattered, somehow, that Kat was innocent of Rex's death, that he had chosen it for himself. It hadn't mattered that he had fought her until he was able to take her knife from her. Kay had watched her, warily, untrusting.

Ell had been sitting in a cushioned window seat, ostensibly looking at a huge picture book but actually, over the top of the page, also watching Kat intensely. The duffel coat she had shed, but her clothes beneath were black, too, and her hair was there in its piles of luxurious, gorgeous sheen. At once Kay had wanted both to lie in it and tear it out by the clump. All three adults (but not Ell) had looked up as the door opened, but they hadn't paused for a moment in the conversation, and Kay and the others had taken seats where they could find them and had listened intently.

"Ghast can't stand against this—not after what happened in Rome—you know that even Foliot will fall from him at the return of the Bride," Will had said. "And with the horn, with the shuttle, with the hall nearly ready—Kat, we have time to hold the Weave *this year*—we can do it in two days."

"We can," said Ned.

"Just about," said Flip.

"Not without the loom," she had concluded flatly, quietly. *"And only a muse may hew the wood whereof the loom is made—* you know the old saying, Will. An instrument like that—"

"We can do it without the loom, Kat, but we can't do it without you." Her father's deep, steady voice took Kay by surprise. She suddenly realized that he must have washed and changed his clothes at Kat's house, putting on his old self as if it were a suit. Now, as he courted Kat's participation in the Weave, he seemed his old self—serious, assured and direct. "We need you to call in all the wispers. Bring them to Bithynia, Kat."

Kay had hated her only for that long moment before she answered; but who could hate a voice like hers that dropped like clumps of soft cream into your ears, its accent like a hot wash that burned the throat of your hearing, but so warmly, as if you couldn't hear the words too slowly? "I don't know," she had said. And then, "A few hours ago I would have happily accepted a tidy commendation from Ghast for bringing Kay in; and now I'm to forget all that? Now I am to forget that Ghast is my master?"

"Yes," Ned More had said. "Forget mastery altogether.

Remember, rather, the thread. Take Kay to Ghast, but take us, too. Call Ghast with his retainers to Bithynia. Let him bring his armies, his bodyguards, his clerks, his private servants. Let them all come. All we need is an instant. Eloise will blow the horn, and Katharine will answer. All the wraiths and phantasms in the Honorable Society will see what we have seen." The fire had caught at all her father's sharpest angles as he spoke, and his face had flickered with its flames. Kay shuddered to remember it. *Two nights*, she had thought.

And she shuddered, too, to remember the messenger who had arrived just at that moment—a terrified, obsequious wraith with a letter in his hand, summoning Kat to a Weave on Ghast's own authority, and commanding her to do exactly what Ned More had—only moments before—been urging her to do in defiance of her master—that is, to call all several hundred wispers to their ancient seats. How Kat had stared at them all in wonder and confusion! How that messenger had looked at them, with fear and distrust! How his eyes had spoken of the horrors that, under Ghast's authority, the whole Society suffered!

But Kat had done it. She had called them all home—century on century of wispers, trailing on their secret paths wheresoever, had answered to her summons. And from the mountain, Ghast, with his armies, his bodyguards, his clerks and his private servants—somehow, they were there.

Phantastes had roused the right-wraiths out of hiding—those that could be found—and from Rome Razzio recalled Oidos, Ontos and the handful of causes who had somehow, miraculously, survived the fire. At the airport Kay and Ell had sat quietly with their father as Flip told a tale or two, and before long the flight crew had made them all at home at the front of a sparsely occupied flight to Istanbul. The girls slept all the way there, and though she'd had a headache as they stepped out into the smoky, dim light of the Turkish airport, Kay hadn't failed to notice the odd tall figure rushing past them, or the odd cloak or robe among the suits and skirts of their fellow passengers. The next day they had rested in the country and made plans—called in favors, arranged for deliveries, and talked and talked as the girls ran wild in a fresh snowfall outside—but on the following morning they had set out again, now by car, for the hall. In a pouch at his waist Will had borne the shuttle. In the sack over his shoulder Phantastes had carried the horn. Flip and Razzio had driven the two cars down the winding, potholed roads. And then they were here.

Here.

There had been no appetite for feasting, no nerves for danc-
ing or for revelry. The command to all had been to assemble, and
the wraiths who now sat around the hall—and Kay could see
them still trickling in—had come to speak, and not to celebrate.
Some faces, she saw, looked hopeful, jubilant, expectant—
these, she supposed, would be the right-wraiths. Rumors had
been passed. Stories had been told. Others seemed more nervous, more fearful, and there were many of them—these, Kay
guessed, were Ghast's servants. Of Ghast there was as yet no
sign, though they had set a chair for him in the center of the
lower part of the hall, opposite the dais. Kay sat in the very
midst of all, on a tiny stool at the midpoint of the hall's long
length, but hard up against the benches of the right-wraiths.
Opposite her, on another stool, Ell perched nervously, holding
Phantastes's sack with the horn within. When the procession
began, Ell knew her part—to blow one long peal on the horn,
and then to wait. She had practiced in the car, very nearly driving them from the road and their senses; but Kay thought now,
with pleasure, that Ell would pull it off perfectly.

To think, she mused to herself again, *we have finally come
to Bithynia.*

The hall was mostly unadorned—only a few banners

hung to each side—and in many places the water and frost damage was severe, and easily seen. Gouges stood out in some of the walls, and the mosaics of the floor were badly cracked or missing in places. But the ceiling was at last intact, and though the place was drafty, it also felt warm, and no rain or snow or wind seeped in through its massive leaded windows. Under heavy clouds, they were almost dark now; just beyond them the weather had turned ever fouler—cold, gusty and sleet-showered. It hardly mattered. With a handful of students and local men, her father had been at work here, off and on, for the better part of a decade—those countless trips and absences, those late nights, all of it poured into Bithynia. Together they had at least made the hall watertight and stopped the rot. In time more banners would hang again from poles anchored in the row of empty wall-slots. In time the floors would be relaid. In time the massive stalls would feel the sharp blades of the master woodcarvers, and the missing diamonds would be reset in the oak lattice of the ceiling. In time the tapestries would come down from the mountain.

But there was one thing, Kay thought with simple happiness as the great curtain at the lower hall was drawn aside, for which they would not have to wait. Six wraiths on either side now bore it up, set on a pallet hoisted with cross-staves, to the top of the hall and set it down. No one knew who had rebuilt it, or how it had been delivered to the hall. Ned More thought perhaps his foreman—who denied it—had had a hand in it, but others ventured that Ghast himself, to mock them, had caused it to be remade, and left for the right time in the vestibule of the Shuttle Hall. However it had gotten there, and whoever had carved and built it, as was the tradition, from solid ash, there it now stood: the great loom of the First Wraith, waxed and set with warp and weft, ready for the consult to begin.

The loom bearers removed their staves and then took their own seats. The heavy green and gold embroidered curtain, five meters across and at least as high, again drew back, and with a start Kay realized that the procession had already begun. It was a simple but a solemn movement down the hall, led by Phantastes and, behind him, one of the lesser imaginers whom he had appointed that day from among the exiled right-wraiths. They wore cassocks of green inlaid with silver, and around their collars tiny diamond studs; their heads were bare. After a short gap, next followed Razzio, leading Oidos and Ontos, all in heavy gowns and black cloaks, with buttons of jet and a single ivory stone set into the cuff at either hand. Behind them, again after a small space, the three youngest of the right-wraiths came in blue cassocks, with gold studs set round their collars; and behind them, last of all, the three youngest left-wraiths, in gray gowns and cloaks, with a black plotting stone threaded into the cuff at either hand, as before. Each of them carried a rod of black iron, its tip embellished with a snake writhing to the point, which was capped with a plotting stone. They came, each of them, without other adornment, and no further ceremony but the stately pace at which they measured the hall, and the register of import that lay graved in their twelve faces; even Phantastes, who had almost gibbered with enthusiasm about the Weave just that morning, stared forward with a resolution that shamed Kay for her delight. She looked down as they approached, and crossed her legs with a scowl.

But at the same moment Ell slid to her feet, and when the twelve, led by Phantastes, stopped just shy of her stool, she lifted the horn to her lips and blew the peal for which she had practiced all that day. Kay had heard the horn before, but not like this—not in this hall, with its huge resound and the amplifying distortion of its wooden ceiling and stalls. It whined like a siren, roared like a lion and wailed like a child all at once, and well before it ended Kay thought her eardrums might bleed

with the singleness of its insistent tone boring into her awareness. All her thoughts lay down and shriveled before the noise.
She watched the sound explode the very air.

Then, as suddenly as it had begun, it ended, and as the
hum and its after-peal rang in the ears of nearly a thousand
wraiths, Phantastes called out to the hall in a resonant bass Kay
had never before heard from him.

"Leap, heart!"

Every wraith in the Shuttle Hall answered him as one.

"The wind will catch you!"

Then the old imaginer led the procession again on its grave
way to the dais. Kay studied them as they passed: Phantastes
with his shining scalp, massive temples, broad shoulders and
thick protruding veins upon his neck; the older right-wraith
with his great eyes like pools, and again the thick blue veins
running across his hands and down his neck; Razzio, Oidos
and Ontos with their olive skin and different heights and gaits;
the younger right-wraiths, again broad and tall, but sallow and
sickly after decades—maybe centuries—in penurious hiding;
and the younger left-wraiths, again short like Razzio, and one
of them very corpulent, but with long, delicate fingers. As these
last passed her, Phantastes had already reached the wheel.

Without breaking step, he advanced to its first position and set his rod into the hole, allowing it to slide heavily through his fingers until with a clang it stood, locked; then he turned and took his place before his throne. The right-wraith behind him took the second position and the seat beside his master, and so, each placing a rod and each choosing a seat, they all completed their procession, the imaginers fanning off to the left, the plotters to the right. When they were all at last standing before their thrones, they sat together in a single motion. A murmur went around the hall, and Kay recognized that the Weave had now officially begun.

"Call the First Wraith!" came a shout from the benches of the right-wraiths, followed by many others, from both sides, clamoring.

Will appeared from the anteroom, adorned in nothing but his old cloak, and walked quickly, even urgently down the length of his hall with no ceremony at all; he even raised his eyebrows, with a little cock of the cheek, as he passed Kay, though he didn't look up from the floor. First he went to the wheel and, grasping two rods in his outstretched hands, ground the huge iron frame along its circular path into its final position.

Twelve nights.

He stood for a moment, looking at it and seeming to draw his breath in dying waves. At the step, then, before the thrones, on one knee he received from Razzio the shuttle; when he reached the loom, he turned to face the hall and held it up before him. At this there was a greater murmur than before. Will held it to his lips and blew a seven-second note—not this time one of the familiar tones, but a new one: low, jarring, but rising and finishing in a keen knife-thrust note as bleak and total as the horn of the Primary Fury. Kay stiffened; she needed no interpreter to tell her that this was the note of tragedy. Now the wraiths in the hall no longer murmured but talked openly, and their voices on both sides sounded distressed—why had the First Wraith chosen the note of the old tragedies? What would befall them all tonight?

"Call the antagonist!" shouted a voice from the benches of the left-wraiths, and though not as many voices as before answered it, still the call was taken up until Ghast himself appeared from the anteroom, his short, squat form dwarfed by the grand drape of the hall curtain. No wonder, Kay thought, Ghast had wanted to get away from this place—it was completely the wrong scale for him. Suddenly, across the hall among the left-wraiths, she picked out Flip sitting beside Kat and, catching his eye, smiled at him. He rolled his eyes; he thought he had an idea of what was coming.

But at the sight of Ghast, a knot had gathered in Kay's stomach. She saw him look out over the hall, and she thought suddenly that his gaze looked *practiced*.

In a flash she saw him walking the length of the hall alone, lamp held aloft in the darkness. She saw him pace the floor, saw him take the seat just opposite her on the bench among the left-wraiths. She saw his thoughts. *My dream. What have we done?* She knew it was no use trying to hold on to a dream, that it surfaced like bubbles in a pond, no sooner visible than vanished. She knew that she could not hold it even now, that it would slip from her fingers the instant she grasped after it. But it was there, that she knew—and her stomach tightened.

Blood spilled on the stone.

"Wraiths and phantasms!" bellowed Ghast. "Many years ago we held what I thought was to be our last congregation in this hall. At your bidding, then, the instruments of the old ways were broken up and scattered, and a new order was spun for the Weave. Since then much has changed, and for the better." He was spitting out his words slowly and clearly, and though he was positioned at the low and far end of the hall, his eyes were roving over the crowded wraiths, taking in as many gazes as he could. Flickers of recognition played across his features as he spoke, and Kay knew he was consummately playing the politician. She watched the wraiths, picking out the few she knew—Foliot, installed at the high end of the hall among the left-wraiths; Kat beside Flip; and on the other side of her, Sprite, by the floor; and Jack, among the stalls at the low end of the right-wraiths. Jack looked worried, Kay thought as Ghast went on.

"For around us, too, the world has changed. Who sits by the fire to drink up the words of the poet? Who pores by weak candlelight over the heavy volumes of the old tales? When was the saga last sung? Who toils through the vedas? What child thinks of Alexander now? Where lie the bones of Gog Magog, or who honors the ashes of the jade queen? These are the lost preoccupations of lesser ages and the dreams of vanished nights. Who knows them now? Scholars!" With theatrical exaggeration, Ghast spat profusely on the floor before him. "Scholars who would sooner own a story than honor it, who would sooner scorn a tale than have skill in it.

"It is the world of women and men that has driven us into the mountain, the world of women and men that has broken the loom, lost the shuttle, crushed the horn and burned the old thread. Some have called me bloody, some ruthless, but the imaginers were not dispersed, nor the right-wraiths scattered by my hand; or if my hand was the instrument, the world of women and men armed me to it." He paused, letting this improbable logic sink in.

Liar.

Kay looked at Will, her eyes asking whether this had not gone on too long; but his face was inclined to the floor, his eyes scattered in the gray arcs of stone that washed across the hall between the benches.

"The stories have all been written," Ghast shouted, "and there is no new thing under the sun! The great tree is dead, and its leaves all are withered! The moors and fens and mountains where once our wispers stalked are farmed, drained and scaled. Why should we walk now by the known ways of the earth, reminding the ungrateful of what they have chosen to forget? We do ourselves dishonor even to think it. There are some who think we must conserve the past and become curators of our vanished glories; but for whose sake shall we rebuild our great library? For whose sake rehang the huge tapestried hall? Surely not for our own.

"No." Ghast was striding the hall now, covering the floor between his low-set seat and the midpoint where Kay perched, increasingly worried, upon her stool. Had he come from the mountain for this? Was this the trap that she had dreamed? Will still hung his head, the shuttle moving absently between his fingers as he sat, eyes averted from the loom. Kay looked to Flip, but he was—strangely—beaming, as if privy to some joke Kay had not yet fathomed. And where was her father? Beyond the windows the meager daylight—which was their only illumination—sagged and darkened, as if on Ghast's cue. He was not speaking now but pacing the hall, searching the faces of the wraiths on both sides, challenging his antagonists to refute him. Had they come to Bithynia for the Bride? his eyes demanded. Did they believe the rumors? Had they really believed for a moment that such a childish myth could *be*?

"The loom has been rebuilt, they say—but by whom, and for what? Indeed it stands before us, and I am grateful that it should be so, and that we should meet in the shadow of its authority. But what should we make upon its great rack now, except the greater sacrifice of our hands? I have heard the horn has been recovered. I have heard the shuttle has been dredged up from the ocean floor. I have heard of jacks and other childish toys, of shellfruits, of blossoms underground—I have heard such whatnots! And to what end? That you should thrall yourselves to the empty ceremonies of the old, dead ways? That you should throw open the doors upon your own tomb, and perish in it?"

Suddenly, and with menacing strides, Ghast covered the half length of the hall, drove directly up to Kay and pointed his stubby, fat finger right in her face. At his height, his eyes were almost level with her own. She recoiled from his curled lip, fearing he would spit upon her. But instead, for the first time that evening he lowered his voice, and spoke directly to her. "You don't believe the hocus-pocus of shellfruits and causes any more than I do. *I* know you. You know what's beneath the House of the Two Modes. You saw the carvings on the walls. You saw the altar. *You* know, as I know, what that house is built on. It is built on *graves*. It is built on nothing but *death*. And through *that* door"—he spun and shouted now at Will, who sat silently with his head bowed—"there is *no passage*." And now he turned back to Kay, and sneered almost down her throat. "In that night there are no stars, only darkness."

Kay's mouth suddenly ran dry as sand, and her stomach collapsed in sickening knots.

"But we have an alternative. We may *manage* our stories. We may *package* them. We may *sell* them. Let us not go back to the Quarries—fine. Let us not go back to the mountain— good. Let us seal it up—excellent. But this place is no more our home now than those craggy voids, for the world of women and men has forgotten it, has thrown it through the door into the bottomless grave of useless history, and if we stay here—if we stay here like this, I say, then we fall with it!"

Ghast stood very close to Kay and let his words sink in for a moment. Then, in a hushed voice, surely almost inaudible to the wraiths sitting at the far reaches of the stalls, he concluded. "Some of you may be surprised to see me here. Perhaps you thought I could not be lured by the trifling tale-telling of our right-handed retroverts. Perhaps you thought I would even now be making good my escape. But I have more respect for the Honorable Society than to think it will submit to these tired old charlatans, to illusionists preaching nonsense about dreams and causes. You, the wraiths of Bithynia, are something more than the playthings of exhausted old traditions. And yet I am glad that we stand here once more, assembled in our ancient home, observing one last time the ancient order, the time-honored ceremonies. Let us resolve once and for all to leave this way. Let us create the forms for a new Weave, a better Weave, a more efficient Weave, a more *prosperous* Weave. Let us do so, and close these doors behind us forever."

Ghast fell silent where he stood, and the whole hall of wraiths on both sides sat speechless, each perhaps waiting for the other to begin. But where the shouts had pealed readily before Ghast's arrival, now Kay thought despairingly that the smiles and bright looks had drooped, and the fixed grimaces of the left-wraiths had hardened. Still Will looked down, and still he turned the shuttle absently in his hands. Meanwhile Ghast walked quietly back to the lower end of the hall. There was a chair there—a plain, everyday chair. Kay wondered that she hadn't noticed it earlier. With one of his meaty hands, he took hold of it by the back, then dragged it, scraping the stone floor, until it rested just beyond the lowest, the humblest of the stalls of the left-wraiths. He stood before it.

"I have spoken," he said at last, and sat.

The walls of stone where, at the ends of the hall, they rose unadorned from the floor to the oak-beamed ceiling were not more silent than the Weave during the long breath that greeted Ghast's conclusion. Kay fought her rising panic as the silence continued and still Will did nothing. Then, suddenly, from a wraith sitting not three meters from her stool, a courage-curdling cry came: "Let him be king!" Kay's heart flooded furiously in her chest as the cry was taken up, and up, all around the hall—first by two or three, then five, then twenty, until hundreds of wraiths began to chant it in a gradually resolving unison. The sense of horror and alienation Kay experienced as, on her stool, she began to fold under the pressure of the chant-ing was absolute. For a long moment she dared not raise her eyes from the floor, even to steal a glance at Will or Flip; but when at last she did, she wished she hadn't.

For Flip was no longer smiling, but was himself chant-ing. Nor was he chanting only, but he began to beat his hands emphatically against the bench before him, in a display of impatience and fury. When Kay sought his gaze, she achieved no recognition; was this, she thought, what it was all for? All the friendship, the betrayals, the reconciliations, the stories, the trust? To bring us to this room, this fate, this event? And still between his hands, almost prostrate, Will turned the shuttle over. With sudden and piercing distress, Kay remembered that, though Ghast had before aspired to a kingship over the Honorable Society, he had been prevented by the necessary form of proceeding: he required an author. Ell sat blinking and terrified on her stool, obviously wanting very much to break across the narrow floor to hide in her sister's arms. She had never looked so small to Kay, or so important.

The next few moments seemed to pass very quickly: Ghast stole over the length of the hall with his chair, placing himself opposite the loom and before the twelve knights; Flip slipped off the benches and delivered a velvet bag to Razzio, which Kay by its size and shape knew must contain a crown; the chanting intensified; and the three youngest left-wraiths, in what must have been a carefully orchestrated abduction, descended off the dais and, processing down the hall, suddenly snatched Ell and returned to the loom, bearing her between their hands. Kay's instinct was to give chase and to free Ell from their grasp by any ineffectual means, but the chanting—and the determined faces of so many wraiths around the hall—cowed her.

As if in a dream, and as the chanting continued, the three youngest left-wraiths deposited Ell on the dais before Razzio who, with his hands upon hers, helped her to lift the crown before the assembly. Flip took a place to the right of the loom, and they all—including Will, who at last and too late lifted his haggard head—turned to watch the proceedings. Ten of the knights sat still enthroned on the dais; only Razzio was on his feet, puffed out with the pride Kay had seen in him on their first arrival in Rome the week before, his chin thrust high into the air and his eyelids heavy upon the sights that did not truly concern him. Kay bored into their hearts as she watched how they betrayed themselves, the story of their trials and travels, the friendships and revelations they had sorrowed and suffered for. Now Razzio himself knelt low to the floor and presented his knee to Ell, gesturing for her to stand upon it and, from above, to place the crown upon the head of the seated Ghast. For his part, his face spoke total command: not a line, not a hairy mole was out of place.

As Eloise lifted the shell-ivory crown, with its elaborate ornament of whorl and plotting stone, delicately into place upon Ghast's head, the chanting erupted into a magnificent, feral cheer. The hair on the back of Kay's neck bristled to hear it, and for the first time that day she felt not anger, but real fear. Ghast stood up to cheers and loud halloos from the hall all around, and stood fixed while the wraiths in company contin-ued to salute him—by no means all, Kay thought as she looked tentatively around, but enough to carry the momentum of a cheer. Enough, she thought, to overpower his opposers.

The greater half of the wraiths in the hall were still

cheering as Flip, dragging Ell by her little hand, walked slowly back from the disregarded loom, past where Kay was sitting, toward the back of the hall. As they approached, Kay felt the full force of loss like a knife twisting in her gut. *It has all been for this. All the searching, all the discovery, all the awful losses and recoveries. After all this, and I have lost her anyway. I had twelve nights to save you all, and on the twelfth, I failed.*

And for a moment she didn't care.

I am too tired.

As Flip neared her, she saw his face. And, from nothing, her heart ignited in a rage. He still wore the same merry but deranged expression, intent and unhinged, but now he stared full in Kay's face as he passed, taking her eyes in a hold that for an instant she thought she couldn't sustain. Everything in her steeled and went cold, and her head felt flattened within by an overwhelming drone that she knew was nothing but the blood surging like ice through her veins.

But then, suddenly, and so quickly that Kay instantly fretted that she had not seen it at all, she thought Flip winked. Kay's thoughts spun. She sat dumb and unmoving—betrayed, reprieved, betrayed again, reprieved again, uncertain whether to collapse in defeat or throw back her shoulders in triumph.

In a moment Flip had disappeared from the hall, and Ell with him, and the cheering began to fall just a little, and then, as if dragged down under its own weight, it died completely. Ghast seemed about to speak; but just as he raised his right hand and took a deep, ponderous breath, the curtain behind Kay was drawn and into the hall strode, very purposefully, her father.

Within fifty long paces, all measured by a shocked silence, he had covered the length of the hall and stood before the loom and the newly crowned king. Without flourish, he sank to one knee, and in a direct address to Ghast requested, without ceremony or form, that the king would upon the festival of his coronation grant him a boon.

Kay could see clearly Ghast's discomfort: he still stood immediately next to the loom, where Will sat, indifferent; the eleven knights still sat enthroned behind him, where Razzio had retaken his seat; and it was obvious to all that he cared little for the petitioner. But, equally, this was to be his first act as king, and Ghast could not afford to trample too roughshod across the goodwill of his subjects. He turned, almost inquiringly, to Razzio, his neck stiffly soldered to his shoulders as if he feared to topple the crown from his fat head. With a wave of his long fingers, Razzio signaled Oidos. She rose. "It is the ancient custom of the Honorable Society that a king of wraiths should not refuse a petitioner in the Weave," she said perfunctorily, and sat.

"Then anything that is mine to give," Ghast replied, with a forced munificence and to all the company of the hall, "upon the day of my coronation I shall bestow without stint."

Ned More had neither flinched nor shaken, even for a moment, throughout this exchange, but still knelt, staring, at Ghast. "I desire then that you should cause me to weep," he said. Ghast stared at him, uncomprehending. "Or if not to weep, then to laugh. Or to fear, to joy, to sorrow, to suffer. Tell me some tale."

Ghast, unnerved, looked again at Oidos, then over at Firedrake. With sudden resolution he said, "I shall call one of my wraiths—"

"No," said Ned More quietly but forcefully. "I ask that it should be you."

Ghast, who had already raised his arm as if to summon one of the lesser left-wraiths to him, slowly allowed it to fall. His face looked ashen. "I will not," he said.

"You must."

Kay hadn't seen the curtains open for a final time. No one had. Nor did any wraith know the voice that spoke those two commanding words—the clear and sonorous treble that sliced through the air like a sword at once rising and falling, striking and parrying; that both pierced the ear with its sudden violence and sheathed itself in the surety of its unimpeachable authority. But Kay knew that voice and, as she turned, tears had already begun to well in her exhausted eyes, and her hands, though she willed them to reach out, to clap, to fall upon that proud figure before her, only hung limp and paralyzed by her sides.

It was her mother.

Mum. I failed. I left you. Mum. Forgive me.

Clare Worth was dressed in the same long green cassock, trimmed with silver and studded with diamonds, that Phantastes also wore. In her hands she held a rod of black forged iron. She held it like a bat, across her body, as if she had come to break with tradition and not to fulfill it—as if at any moment she might stalk down the hall with her rod ready and begin to swing it. She stared at the wraiths around her, turning her head with a measured sweep to take in first the assembled left-wraiths, then the whole body of right-wraiths, and at last the eleven knights assembled on the dais at the far end of the hall—and, last of all, Ghast upon his throne, as well as her husband, still patiently kneeling before him. Unlike everyone else in the hall, he had not turned round or even flinched at the sound of this new voice. Kay stared hard at his back, uncertain if it was tight with anger or loose with relief.

And then, with firm and unhurried steps, Clare Worth began to walk the length of the hall. The eye of every wraith followed her. Every breath drew even with her steps. Every heart sped to see the iron rod in her hands, that staff lost for a thousand years, for two thousand, for as long as a story can be told or a great imagining conjured. When she reached the hall's end, she hoisted the rod erect in her hands, holding it above her head—and then, with purpose, drove it home into its ancient slot at the head of the great wheel.

Kay lurched breaths. She had seen what she could not dare know, what she could not understand—the head of her mother's iron staff, unlike all the others in this, that it was tipped with gold.

It was you. All along, you. In the sewers at Alexandria. You who saved me on Naxos. It was you with the kermes book. It was you in the catacombs. All along it was you.

Phantastes stood, and stepped forward from his throne.

My mother. You built the loom. Scheherazade.

"My lady," he said, and bowed. Even from where she sat, Kay could see the tears streaming down Phantastes's suddenly haggard cheeks.

Clare ignored him. It was as if she hadn't even heard him. Her hands still grasped the iron rod where she had completed the circle. The room paused. The very air seemed unsure, and faltered. Her eyes were fixed on something distant, or something long ago, as if she were gathering her strength from somewhere great and far off.

Suddenly, with a heave and a terrible cry, Clare Worth pulled back with all her strength on the iron rod in her hands. Kay thought for a second that she had bent it—but no, it wasn't that. The rod, it appeared, was a kind of lever and, as her mother pulled on it, it declined from the center of the circle with a hard, grating sound, as of iron drawing against stone, or a plow cutting into rocky ground—and then rested, fixed and splayed. Clare Worth proceeded around the wheel, heaving on the rods one by one until they had all opened like petals, away from the center of the circle. And with the last, almost like magic, the iron wheel opened at its hub, and from a circular boss she retrieved a huge, luminous dark-blue stone. Cupping it with both hands, she carried it down the length of the hall.

"Mum," said Kay. "It's Ell—they took her, I couldn't—"

"I love you," said Clare to Kay, placing the stone in her outstretched palms. Their eyes met in a fathomless tenderness, but she did not smile. "Don't go running off again."

In the utter hush she recrossed the length of the hall. The knights stood as she approached, making way for Clare Worth to assume the throne of honor at their center, and then together the twelve of them took their seats. Ghast stared at them, at Kay, and with obvious terror at the heavy blue gem in her hands, which seemed to glow within its rounded surface with the white lines of a twelve-pointed star.

Stars were there.

Ghast had gone gray with fear. But that, Kay thought, was nothing compared to the pallor that swept across his features as Will—without prologue or demonstration—slipped the pirn into the shuttle, then began to set the threads upon the loom. After so many years, he would have a story at last.

"Tell your story, Ghast of the Bindery, King of Wraiths and Phantasms." Clare Worth put her hands on the arms of her throne and closed her eyes. "Tell your story and grant your boon."

After a painfully protracted silence, during which not a single wraith so much as cleared her throat, Ghast began.

"There was once a man. All his desire was to be great. He would achieve great things, but he had neither skill nor knowledge. He had no aptitude, no opportunity. For years he woke, ate, did unmemorable things, repeated them, ate again, slept; and he hid his desire for greatness in the darkest corner of his awareness. He hid it because, as an ambition he could not fulfill, it only caused him pain. The years accumulated and grew upon him like earth, weighing him down, driving ever further into the cold, airless, lightless past his sacred hunger. If he had recalled his youthful ambition, he would have found that his appetite for greatness had dulled with the gradual accomplishment of mean honors, with the acquisition of almost useless abilities—but he never had the leisure to consider himself, and ever less as his authority widened, the demands on his schedule multiplied and the number of his clients grew."

The words were produced slowly, but not haltingly. Like them all, Kay could see that this kind of speaking did not come easily to Ghast, and yet his features and the tension in his frame as he spoke seemed to betray not only uneasiness, but a kind of contemptuous intensity. Before him, though completely disregarded, her father still knelt, impassive.

"The day came when other men might have crossed that invisible threshold, passing from a life of patient, pointless toil to a retirement of unremarkable senility. But this man discovered, to his surprise, that the world around him had shrunk, withered, decayed. The skills he had once sought and failed to achieve; the knowledge he had once sought to master, but staggered in; the opportunities that he had once so fervently coveted, but missed—these now had vanished from the world. Little by little the ambition and hunger that had relentlessly dogged his youngest years fought their way to the surface of his being and his doing, and he began to discover—though only by glimpses at first—that all he required to differentiate himself from and, indeed, to prefer himself to the world was his pure ambition. The hunger alone would set him apart. In very little time he was reputed the greatest man then living, and so achieved his desire."

That can't be all. That can't be the best you can do. Even you.

There Ghast ended, punctuating his speech with a defiant stare not only at Edward More, but at the assembled wraiths on both sides of the hall, whose expectation had demanded, and secured, this demeaning display from him. And well might he defy them, Kay thought, for his story had been awful, mean, pointless and empty; and as she followed his eyes to those of his audience, she saw in them the same distrust, the same dissatisfaction, the same contempt that he reflected back at them; nor was this among the right-wraiths only, but even the left-wraiths, and even those who only a short while before had chanted most enthusiastically, Ghast's brief, incompetent and vicious display met with less than a resigned disbelief. It had aroused their impatience, their shame and even (as Kay watched the faces, and the minds that made the faces) their hatred. Ghast had ended, and the hall fell not silent, but uncomfortably, simmeringly void. Rustling, stamping and the clearing of throats began menacingly to emanate from the right of the hall, and from its left a shamed defiance. Kay could sense the coming confrontation, though it was not yet clear whether it would conclude as cooperation or an outright brawl.

And then Ghast began again to speak—or so Kay thought, until, reverting to him, she found his lips still and his features verging on a poorly concealed rage. She couldn't see, couldn't hear whence the voice came, but it was scored and stippled out with the faint beat of a tapping drum—and though it rose and fell like a wave rolling, or like a thread passing in and out of the texture of the weave, it always moved, was always there, full of forward motion. In a clap of stunned recognition, Kay realized that it was Will's voice, and that he had taken up the story while he worked at it himself upon the loom.

"This was the man of despair who, like Phaethon, the child of the sun-god Helios, attempted in his greed to seize and control that which lay beyond him—and, in reaching for it, destroyed it. Phaethon, disregarded boy, who was not content to remain one of the blessed children of the sun, to wear his father's livery on his cheek or upon his shoulders; Phaethon, who could not rest in his thought until he had caught the very reins in his hand, until he had put the horses under his sole direction, until he had seized his father's chariot and driven the sun almost into the earth. Cruel and catastrophic ambition! The fertile vines of Italy and Greece burst into flame, and the vineyards, laid waste, became deserts; the sea like a pot set upon a stove bubbled and steamed, and then boiled dry; the trees grown torches, the fields grown sheets of fire, burned, and upon them the people ran like whole, searing blisters, their eyes frying in their sockets and their skin pouring from their charring bones like fast-melted wax. Who heard the cries of children among the bellowings of oxen and horses, among the screams of plummeting eagles? Happy then were those who chanced before the relentless ball of flame to fall into some deep pool or flooded cavern, where they might shelter awhile from the blast! Happy then were the worms, the moles, the badgers and the foxes that by burrowing in the cool soil and clay seemed to evade the scorching flames that fell from the air! Happy then were all those towering birds of prey that in the high mountains sought out ice and snow in which to save themselves! But pools were blasted away, the very clay was baked into dust, and the mountains stripped bare but for the drifting heaps of ash that once had been forests. Small wonder, then, that while the world burned, the father of the gods whetted his titanic bolt and, hurling it, dashed Phaethon from the sky and scattered him in pieces upon the earth.

"So was the world and all that was in it brought to destruction by a childish overreaching, a greed born of despair, that would rather kill the thing it desires, than allow others to enjoy it. It is a story as old as stories are, told by every people, a memory of the great cataclysms of the past and a prophecy of those to come. But it is not the last story; for always when the selfish appetite, overrunning everything, has consumed itself and fed at last upon its own ruin, then other voices, perhaps quiet at first, can be heard; then other feet, light steps though they may be, tread the embers and from the ashes begin again to raise a harvest. The daughters of Helios, in grief for Phaethon, their brother, scoured the plains and shores of Italy to collect the pieces of his thunder-torn corpse. Piece by piece they composed him, a work of years, until they were able to give him burial, their brother, the companion of their mother's womb, their blood and their flesh, at last laid to rest. But in their mourning, in their sad and weary steps as they brought his body to the grave, they also created something new: no sooner had they poured funeral libations upon his scattered corpse, no sooner had they cast handfuls of earth upon his body, no sooner had they with tears and laments sounded the last of his days, than the gods caused thin webs to spin along their palms and fingers, transforming them into leaves, while a crusty bark ramified each limb, stretching and branching it into a network of trunk, bough, twig and stem. From their feet, where they stood along the banks of the river Eridanus, roots crawled into the earth, binding them to the shore, while from their eyes tears like thick slugs of amber dropped into the water below, as still they do today.

"In the same way Isis, goddess of the moon, soaked all Egypt in her tears when, after the death of her husband, Osiris, she roamed the valley of the Nile, seeking the scattered pieces of his body. With his death, the great light of the sun had been extinguished; all Egypt surrendered to flood, to rot and to plague; and it seemed as if every good of the world would be drowned in the relentless waves of the spreading river. But in her grief Isis told another tale, and as she gathered here an arm, there a finger, here the hip of her beloved and there a rib, piecemeal she reconstructed her lord and husband, until the day when, through her devotion and determination, he sat again upon the royal throne at Abydos, dispensing justice. It is said that this queen of Egypt breathed life into her dead and dismembered lord not merely by her laments, her tears or her faith, but by her stories: myths of Osiris's great acts dropped from her mouth as she trod her pilgrim way; myths and legends, the histories of his ancestors, the tale of his miraculous birth, his attributes and his life, word after word knitted like the stitches wherewith surgeons bind flesh on flesh to heal the ragged wound. So by telling him over, she gathered him together. So by telling over his story, even now, we, too, not only remember him and her, the tale together with its teller, but also breathe into them both new life, and renew our own.

"For which poet, which teller of stories, is not also a healer? Which ballad-maker is not likewise a priest, who in laying on the hands of a parable brings the dead again to life? To spin a yarn, as the singer Orpheus knew, is to go to hell for your bride—as Orpheus himself did when the gods moved the venomous snake to strike the heel of his beloved Eurydice. Orpheus braved the gods, charming the three-headed dog of the underworld, Cerberus, and seducing the ear of horrid Persephone, queen of Hades, before he might in triumph lead his bride again toward the light. So, even in death there is life, even in the end there lies a beginning, even from ashes a conquest may rise. Then let fall your tears of amber, O you daughters of Helios! Drop here and there your quickening stories, Isis, faithful queen! And you, Orpheus, great singer of tales, go you to hell and ransom the fair Eurydice—for while I weave, the Bride still whispers among the groves of old Bithynia!"

Kay knew as soon as the last word was pronounced that it had happened again: she must have slipped, mesmerized, into that same trance she had experienced in Paris three days before, because she now stood not before her chair or in the middle of the hall, but at its end, just before the dais and adjacent to the loom itself, which still worked quickly, weaving, under the hands of the First Wraith. In her cupped hands lay the Bridestone, faintly glowing, its star the quiet, still promise of a new birth; in Will's hands the shuttle, by contrast, moved like a wild and a live thing. He was nowhere near completion, but the beginnings of the tapestry had started to take color under his hands as the shuttle wove through the threads with such speed that the air, rushing through it, created a low hum from every one of its tiny apertures: a quiet music, whistling and droning from Will's light grasp as he worked. Kay watched his delicate fingers threading in the total silence of the hall. She knew, this time, what had shocked the wraiths, and why they now sat so still. She knew what momentous heavings were stirring in their conscious thoughts, but strangely this understanding of their gravity seemed to free her from it, and she was all witness to Will's working, and she loved the dance of his hands among the thread, the way his fingers hardly touched the shuttle at all—as if they held, rather, all the air around its quick ovular sheen, and didn't so much push it through the warp as guide the places where it might no longer be. It was a negative moment, a play of space and gap, a dance between forms.

But the movement of the shuttle was not all; there was, too, the hard pressure of the bar, and the relentless closing up of space between the threads—and the bar worked like a lung, yawning open to free the hands, then slamming closed to build the weave, then open again, then closed. The voice of the shuttle moved murmuring in among these long breaths, with the lesser music of words weaving in the line, stringing in the fabric of the weft. Kay knew then that the origin of the poetry she had been sung all her life lay in this cross-woven fabric of depth, of motion, time and color, as the shifting weight of recognition turned over, behind her, in hundreds on hundreds of minds, like the upending of some great mass in the sea. And she was conscious then of another sound, which was nearby and completely unlike the silence, completely unlike the blurred chaos of the shuttle; it pealed raspingly, like the death to which it was the prelude. Kay didn't need to look behind her to know that Ghast now lay upon the stone floor of the hall, or that the little rhythm of flecking hisses she heard was his last breath escaping between his foamy lips. There would be no saving him. Kay felt neither sorry nor glad; she simply felt the open and closing of the bar as it moved across the gaps of threading fingers. Within the black border that would run all around the final work, she had known what the image would be, and she smiled now to see the face of Eurydice emerging, wreathed with serpents.

There was but one thing remaining. Kay knew just how it would be. She turned to face the silent hall, and the eyes of the whole Honorable Society of Wraiths and Phantasms settled upon her. She was still smiling. Almost as one, every wraith in the hall turned to follow her own gaze toward the far entrance, where Ell's face suddenly appeared, draped in the embroidered green velvet that still curtained her little body.

"Mum!" she shouted, and the peal of it rang across the ranks of wraiths as a ripple spreads on water, washing every face with the joy of return, of renewal, of rebirth. Ell broke through the curtains and ran the length of the hall, her feet stamping upon the mosaics—and, threading the rods, straight across the opened flower of the wheel. And the centuries of wraiths where she passed rose as one to their feet. And as she threw herself into her mother's outstretched arms, every one of their voices—with the very stones and glass, the wood and each painted ornament that decked the ancient hall, still rocking to the beat of the working loom—exploded into song.

Epilogue

The fingers moved across the piano keys like a rippling wave over pebbles. Kay watched them roll and then, by little leaps, spring up and down across the arpeggios, or fan to collect distributed chords. Her mother's hands were long and slender, with no apparent cast of muscle to them at all; and yet she could make the little room throb with the sound of a handgrip. Nor did she ever look down at them as they wheeled, eddied, pounced, twirled and wove across the keyboard, instead keeping her eyes firmly fixed on the score flung open on the rack before her. It was almost as if she were two people, and not one: a watcher with her eyes, and a doer with her hands.

Just as the long waltz fell into the last of its cadences, there was a little tap at the study door.

"I'm just heading into work," her father said. He already

had his knapsack over his shoulders, but was still holding an empty mug of coffee. Kay held out her hand, and took the mug when he handed it to her. He looked confused, as if he didn't quite remember having picked it up.

"And you'll be back when?" said her mother. It wasn't a question; it was a challenge, as ancient and as formal as the trumpet sounded before a tournament.

"Not a minute after five."

"Good, because we've set aside the whole night for gifts, and for being together."

Kay let slip her pent breath.

Dr. Edward More smiled and tapped his temple with his forefinger. "I've been thinking of nothing else," he said. He turned toward the front door, taking a couple of strides, and they braced themselves for the careless way in which he tended to let it slam behind him, so forcefully that the whole house, with all its windows and joists and loose change, seemed to rattle. Kay knew it set her mother's teeth on edge. And now, in the even winter light, the air around them still threaded with those strings of melody and harmony, it would break the spell completely.

But he didn't go out. Instead, he put his head back through the study door again.

"Have you looked at that little book Eloise is making?" he asked. She was upstairs, ensconced in a cluttered den she had made in their bedroom, scribbling furiously in a kind of notebook she had fashioned from scraps, and cuttings, fabric, glue and string. She had been at it for days.

"It's really something," he added. Kay watched her mother looking at her father. She didn't say a word, but a softness poured out of her eyes, and pooled in her cheeks, and in her mouth. Her face was a music.

"Love you both," said her father, and then he was gone. The door clicked on the latch like a robin lighting on a ledge.

The music had not been broken. Its moment hung around them, still, like a soft, desired veil. Kay bounced a little onto her toes and, from her patient stand next to the higher registers, she cleared her throat.

"Mum?"

"Yes, Katharine." Clare Worth placed her hands exactly on her thighs, and swiveled upon her stool so as to face her daughter.

"Do you ever look at your hands while you're playing the piano?"

"Not for a long time, Katharine. Why?"

"They remind me of something. Well, of two things actually."

Clare Worth was silent, and Kay wasn't sure that she even took a breath.

Outside, a wood pigeon found its throat, but her mother just regarded her, calmly, staring directly into her eyes; and for a moment Kay felt as if a hood had been drawn up over all the world but this one face, which lay revealed to her in all its simplicity and ancientness, its inarticulate kindness, its mathematical materiality.

Plotting. Imagination.

"By the muses, they remind me of those things too, Kay," said Clare Worth at last. Without another word, she stood and lifted the cover of the huge piano, drawing up the prop to set the cover open. With the same quiet delicateness, she removed the music stand and all its furniture. When she had exposed the sounding board, and above it all the instrument's strings and hammers, then she sat down and began again to play from the beginning—and while the music whorled and threaded, the two of them poured their mutual gaze upon her long and agile, loom-building fingers.